Missing Pieces

Guardian Security Book Six

by

Desiree Holt

Missing Pieces

Contact Information: info@thewildrosepress.com

Cover Art by *Diana Carlile*

The Wild Rose Press, Inc.
PO Box 708
Adams Basin, NY 14410-0708

Publishing History
First Edition, 2022
Print ISBN 978-1-5092-4426-3
Digital ISBN 978-1-5092-4427-0

Published in the United States of America

Could he save the woman he loved and the child he just discovered before it was too late?

"Hold on." Ethan held up a hand. "There's a few things to get straight first."

"Like what?"

"Like the fact that Jen came here because she's more concerned about her daughter's safety—your daughter's—than anything else. But there's a problem."

Dino quirked an eyebrow. "Worse than it already is?"

"Let's go inside and let me explain. But first you should know that Jen took off."

Dino stopped as if his feet had grown into the ground. "She took off? As in left?"

Could this possibly get any worse?

Ethan nodded. "Jen always was able to memorize things. She must have watched me punch the code to close the gate when she got here, because this morning, she opened it and drove away."

"Drove away?" Dino had a hard time holding onto his temper. "She managed to get away from the great Ethan Caine?"

"Don't rub it in," he griped. "Lisa already beat you to it. And yes, right under my nose. But she left a note."

"Oh, great. Fantastic. Where the fuck is it?"

"I've got it, but let's go inside before I give it to you. You'll need a lot of coffee for this one."

"Wait. Where's the kid?"

Ethan sighed. "Here. With us. And quit referring to her as the kid. She's your flesh and blood."

But calling her that kept his emotional armor on place in case this was a disaster.

Dino stared at him. "She left her? Just left her? Here? What the hell?"

"It's all in the note. Come on."

"Fine. Lead the way." He was still trying to control his anger, although he wasn't sure who he was angry at, Jen or himself. And the mixture of emotions flooding him knocked him off balance. "Let's see what the fuck she's gotten herself into."

Dedication

To my team: Maria Connor, Steven Horwitz, beta
reader Margie Hager and of course my incredible
editor, Diana Carlile and The Wild Rose Press,
which has been my home since
my first book was written.

Chapter One

A suburb of Detroit, Michigan

Jennifer LaCroix took a breath in an attempt to still her galloping pulse and get herself under control. What an unbelievable mess this was. And just how had it all ended up in her lap, anyway? It had to be Sutherland, that jerk, pointing his finger in her direction. She'd never liked him or trusted him, not in all the years she'd worked at the museum, and now she had even more reason not to.

Chaos reigned all around her. A shipment of antiquities, the largest yet, was scheduled to arrive at the museum for a special show. They'd be on display for three months, thanks to the owner who'd loaned them, and the entire shipment had somehow disappeared. Craig Sutherland, the museum director, swore he'd never signed for them, but the shipping company driver insisted he had. Meanwhile, they were missing.

In the ten years Jen had worked here, she'd never seen such pandemonium. But of course, a disaster like this had never happened before, either. When the discovery was made three days ago that the latest shipment of artifacts had gone missing, everyone went crazy. Of course, they did. Those artifacts were rare and uber costly. Some even said priceless. Crazy was a mild term for how it had been since then. FBI agents were all over the place, and the museum board was everywhere, scrutinizing everyone and everything. Giving everyone the third degree.

The board was also doing its best to clamp a lid on things, because if the owners of the artifacts heard, there'd be ten kinds of hell to pay. The blowback might even cause the museum to close. The story was all over the media, the board was in an uproar, the staff was in a panic.

Sutherland was sweating bullets, despite his efforts to maintain control. Major donors were involved in the museum, many of them thanks to his efforts. If they all pulled their support, the place would definitely close. No wonder Roger Welborn, the chairman of the board of directors of the museum, was raising holy hell and rightfully so. He was angrier than she'd ever seen him. It was almost as if they'd been stolen from him personally. Thank the lord, at least, he wasn't here today, throwing his weight around, telling her how the museum was his responsibility and if she knew anything at all, she'd better tell him or get herself a good lawyer.

Sutherland, who was also her immediate boss, still denied any involvement, of course. Said he hadn't even been at the museum the day the shipment arrived. That it was scheduled for a different day. The driver was now nowhere to be found, and the signature on the receiving form was totally illegible.

And now, here she was, headed yet again for the room the federal agents were using. Why? She'd already told them everything she knew at least five times. Answered their questions a million times. But the damn suits had summoned her for questioning yet again. Summoned!

Her throat was dry, but her palms were sweaty as hell. Nausea gripped her and she prayed she didn't throw up. Why did the Feds want to ask her more questions? Was she being targeted to take the fall? Why? And by whom?

What the hell was going on?

Rumors were flying. Craig wasn't exactly popular with the employees, so pointing the finger at him for this was a natural reaction. Some even said he'd gotten his tail in a financial crack and selling the antiquities was his best answer. Jen certainly knew there were enough uber wealthy people out there who would pay big bucks for the stuff, stolen or not. There was speculation that if it was him, he was planning to disappear and leave this mess in someone else's lap.

Would it be hers? Had he dumped it on her? Was that why the FBI said they wanted to question her again?

She had done her best to keep a low profile. The delivery had gotten screwed up somehow. That's all she could think of. Usually there were guards in the delivery truck and a museum guard to assist with the receipt of the items. None of that had happened. Sutherland was claiming the delivery date was changed, and that she, Jen, must have done it to get her hands on the items. That was the only answer he could think of.

What bothered her was how quick people were to believe it. Not that she'd spent any time cultivating friendships at work. She'd done her job, done it well, and devoted the rest of her time to Deanne. Still, she would have thought someone would wonder why a woman who worked hard and kept her nose clean was being accused of this.

Her stomach had been tied in knots for three days as she was questioned over and over and over. And now they had sent word they wanted to talk to her again. Again! God! Had Craig weaseled out by dumping this whole mess on her? She had to talk to him before she met with the Feds again.

As she approached his office, she heard his voice.

"Don't threaten me, asshole."

Jen LaCroix sucked in a breath and stopped where she stood, absolutely still, listening to his voice. Apparently, he'd thought he'd closed his office door all the way, but it was open a tiny crack, just enough so she could hear him. Through the thin opening, she saw him standing at his desk, talking on his cell phone. Frozen in place, she strained her ears to hear him, hoping no one came by here. Who on earth could he be talking to? She held her breath and pressed against the tall pieces of statuary right outside his door.

"That's what I said, Welborn."

Welborn? The chairman of the board? Surely, he didn't have anything to do with this. Right?

"I don't do well with threats. I told you this entire shipment had disappeared along with your special items, so I have nothing for you. I already have enough trouble from this. There's nothing for you this time, and plus, the situation has made it impossible for us to continue our arrangement. Too many eyes on me."

They had to be discussing the missing shipment. Nothing else made sense. It was all anyone was talking about. No one had yet been able to locate the mysterious person who had received it and whose signature was unrecognizable. It was now in the wind.

Craig, as the museum director, always received the shipments and signed for them. This time, or so he claimed, he'd been out when the boxes arrived, and he had no idea who signed for them. Didn't even know they'd arrived, or so he said. She personally had no clue what had happened to it. What on earth was included with it that Roger Welborn had a special interest in? What did he have to do with it? There had to be something about this shipment that caused it to go missing.

Was it all a big lie? But it was Welborn who called in the FBI. Welborn who was raising holy hell. Welborn who had everyone running around like their hair was on fire. So what did he have going on with Sutherland that no one could find out about?

"Listen to me." Sutherland's voice had a grating sound. "For five years, I've been locating items for you and paying people to hide them in shipments to the museum. If I hadn't been sucker enough to get pulled into your poker game, I wouldn't be in this position."

Holy shit! Five years? What did he mean? And what poker game?

Jen wondered if he meant the ones Welborn hosted privately that people speculated about. They involved people with a lot of power or money or both.

"No, damn it, I already told you ten times I don't have them," Sutherland snapped. His next words sent a chill racing down her spine. "I told you, I told the Feds, and I'll tell you again. Take a look at snotty Jen LaCroix who's thought she was too good for all of us from the day she got here. She's got a kid to support and no husband. I'd put money down that she figured out how to grab it while I was out and has it hidden somewhere until she can figure out how to sell it. Maybe she already has a buyer. No, I'm not asking her. Are you crazy? Ask her your damn self. Yes, the FBI's asked to talk to her again. Take it up with them."

She sucked in a breath. What was he doing to her? He'd begun to resent her the past few years, mostly because she studied her craft and knew more about the antiquities coming into the museum than he did. And because the board members had begun to look at her with more respect and attention than they gave to him.

The last thing she wanted was to call attention to herself. What if somehow word got to Dino? What if— Oh, god!—he saw a picture of her and Deanne somehow and recognized the girl as the daughter he didn't even know he had. For a moment, she was afraid she'd throw up right where she stood.

"What?" Craig's voice had lowered. "Unless she already got rid of them, if she has them anywhere, she's got them at her house. She's got that nice little place just at the edge of town, situated among all those trees. It's almost as if she planned this from the beginning and rented the house because it was a good place to hide things. No, I have no idea, but I'll tell you this. I can't be mixed up in something getting this much publicity. I've had enough. I'm done. I'm getting in my car, going home, making arrangements for my wife, and getting the fuck out of here. What do I care what everyone thinks?'

There was silence for another minute, and she was almost ready to ease herself away from his office, but his next words stopped her. This time his tone was different.

"That money's mine. I earned it, and you'd better leave me the fuck alone. Listen," Craig continued, "I have to get the hell out of here before they really start digging. If they find our connection, we'll both be in deep shit, you more than me. This is over with. My debt is paid, and I'm done."

Another pause.

"Maybe it's a sign that our business arrangement really does need to come to an end. I told you I can't keep doing it. No, I'm done with that, too. I have to get out from under this. I can't live like this any longer."

The pause this time was even longer.

"What? No, no, no. I told you, damn it. I do not have any of it. God knows I almost got my nuts in a wringer because of our arrangement, and that's why I'm done. I'm getting the fuck out of here while I can. Don't look for me." There was a long moment of silence, during which Jen wondered if he'd just hung up. "Yes," he said at last. "Yes, I'm sure Jen's got them. That's the only possible answer. I told you, I hinted as much to the Feds to point them in that direction and away from me."

Jen thought she might faint. No wonder the FBI wanted to talk to her again.

"What? How? Damn it. I'm not saying it again. I wasn't here when the shipment arrived. She could have intercepted this delivery and claimed it never arrived. If you want to find your stuff, check out that woman's house."

Oh, god! He'd painted a damn bullseye on her back. Jen swallowed hard. She had to fight the urge to barge into his office and smack the little shit.

"What? You think I'm an idiot? Of course I did.

Told them, regretfully, much as I didn't want to believe it, she had to be the one. I'd heard she really needed the money. Hinted she might even have been smuggling goods in this way for a while and selling them. This time she probably took the museum stuff, too. Shocked, of course, that she might do such a thing. You know the drill. I had to make sure they were off my back, for which you should be grateful."

Holy shit! Jen nearly fainted at that, every bit of saliva in her mouth drying up.

"What? No, of course not." He raised his voice. "Damn it, I said no. I can't do that. I have to leave. This is all caving in on my head. No, I never should have gone to the damn poker game to begin with."

There was a longer moment of silence now, during which Jen wondered if Sutherland had just hung up on the call. But then he spoke again.

"No. It was my damn ego, puffed up because the fucking chairman of the fucking museum board invited me to his private game. I'm wondering if the whole thing was a setup from the beginning. Doesn't matter now, though. I can't do it anymore. We're finished. You and I have to get the fuck away from here. We're done. I mean it. Just forget my name."

He must have been doing this a long time, whatever it was. He controlled all the shipments to the museum and was certainly in the best position to make it happen. And what was he selling illegally if the legitimate shipments were safely logged in? The biggest shock was discovering that Roger Welborn was apparently involved in this with him. She'd heard the man was a big collector, but would he be involved in something like that?

Her answer was, absolutely. The guy was a wealthy asshole who used people to his advantage and didn't think rules applied to him.

"I'm telling you for the last time. Leave me alone. Go to her house. She probably thinks they're safe there until she can do whatever with them."

Another pause.

"Yes. That's what I said. Send someone to her house now while she's still in her office here. You'd better get your own ass in gear because the Feds will be on the way as soon as their warrant comes through. No, I can't. I have to go. Now. I'm hanging up this minute. I'm done. This is getting to be too much of a mess for me. Be grateful you got what you did, but I'm out of here. Going where no one will find me."

Holy shit!

How had all this happened practically under her nose, and she hadn't seen it? She counted to ten, waiting for Sutherland to finish his call. But before she could move, she heard his voice again, lower this time and apparently on another call.

"It's me. Yes, it's still crazy around here, but I can't wait any longer to leave. While Jen's tied up with the Feds, I can just ease out of here. Yes, I've made all my arrangements. We've been over this again and again. You've got the cell phone I gave you? Okay, just do what we said. And keep putting on that good act for the Feds and everyone. Yes, I'll let you know when I get there. We've already made plans for you so just keep doing what you're doing. Yes, I love you, too. Be careful."

He grabbed his briefcase and headed for the door. She hid behind the statue outside the door to his office while he raced to get the hell out of there. Where was he going in the middle of all this chaos? The museum was his responsibility, so why was he ducking out? He was obviously the one who'd done this.

Should she go talk to the Feds? Would they believe her if she told them what she'd just overheard? Not if their attitude toward her was any indication. What if they arrested her? What would happen to Deanne? Oh, god. Her stomach cramped at the thought. She had to get out of here. Get away. Protect herself and her child. Hide somewhere until this all blew over if it ever did.

She tried to quiet her racing heart enough to make her own escape without being seen. She hurried away from Craig's office, shaking as she fast-walked out to her car.

Pick up Deanne. Get home. Pack. Get the hell out of here. She'd figure out where to go after that.

She raced through traffic, driving as fast as she could to where Deanne was spending the day with a friend and practically yanked her away. Welborn had her name, and who knew what the hell he would do if he got hold of her. Getting out of town and hiding somewhere was the only answer.

Damn it!

Her cell phone rang as she drove, but she refused to answer it, instead letting it go to voice mail. She punched the button to hear the message over the speaker. She recognized the voice as the chairman of the board.

"Jennifer, this is Roger Welborn."

Chairman of the museum board. And obviously somehow involved in this mess. Oh, god. She couldn't talk to him. She had to get her stuff and Deanne's and get away from here as fast as she could.

"I hate to do this over the phone, but you left me no choice, disappearing the way you did. The FBI is not pleased with the way you ran out on their interview, and it doesn't look good for you. I need to understand what your involvement in all this is, so we need to meet immediately. I know the Feds want to see you again right away, so get back here now. Call me immediately. If I don't hear from you, I'm sure the FBI will be sending people out to look for you. This is a serious matter."

That was an understatement.

Jen hit the Off button. She'd delete the voice mail message when she got to the house. The man wielded a lot of power. If he needed a scapegoat, Craig Sutherland had handed them the perfect one in her. And for whatever reason, the wife of the board chairman did not like her. Even if her innocence was proven, she could end up losing her job and maybe even going to jail just on circumstantial evidence.

She'd left so much behind when she fled another different situation ten years ago, but it had worked out well. Life here had been good, quiet, uneventful, or at least she thought so. Now, thanks to Craig Sutherland, it was all up in smoke. She needed a safe place for Deanne and then somewhere she could disappear until this was all sorted out.

"But why are we in such a hurry," her daughter kept asking as she drove toward the house like a maniac. "Where are we going? What's wrong, Mom?"

What's wrong? Everything. How dare he put me and Deanne in jeopardy to save his own skinny ass?

"Everything's okay, sweetheart, but we're taking a

long trip. And you're going to meet someone who is going to help us."

"Help us with what?"

"There are some bad people who think I have something that belongs to them. I don't, but I don't want to be around to argue with them."

"But where are we going?" her daughter asked again.

"Someplace you'll like. I promise."

Someplace where you'll be safe.

The house she'd been renting was just outside of town on a short road, surrounded by clusters of trees. She liked it because it made her feel as if they were living in their own cocoon. She had pretty much limited her social contacts, although she made sure Deanne had a busy, active life.

She parked the car away from the house, hiding it in the thicket of trees, then hustled her daughter inside. The first thing she did was take her little SIG P365 from the small safe in her closet and put it on her bed. When she'd first landed in Michigan, she'd decided, living alone and knowing nobody, she needed protection. Lessons at the local gun range had taken care of that. At least she'd have security of some kind in this situation. She'd also taken some self-defense classes, telling herself a woman alone couldn't be too careful. Whatever happened, at least she'd be able to protect herself.

She began packing the suitcases she'd dragged out of the big closet. Deanne said nothing, just helped by bringing her own things into the bedroom. They had filled three of the suitcases and were working on the fourth when Jen heard a car pull up in the driveway.

The doorbell rang, followed by the sound of breaking glass.

Oh, god.

They hadn't wasted any time. She shoved the suitcases back in the closet, stuck the gun in her pocket and turned to Deanne.

Please, god, let us get out of here before whoever Sutherland sent shows up.

"Deanne, you know I love you, right? Please just do what I say, don't ask questions, and everything will be all right."

Maybe.

At that moment, the front door opened, and heavy footsteps sounded through the downstairs.

Oh, god. Please don't let them find us.

Chapter Two

"Come on," she whispered to Deanne. "We're going to play a little game, sweetie. Kind of like Hide and Seek."

Deanne looked at her, fear bright in her eyes. "But—"

"Please, baby. Just do as I ask, okay?"

"Okay," Deanne whispered.

"Shh." Jen pressed a finger to her lips. "We have to be absolutely quiet. Can you do that?"

Deanne, who looked scared to death, nodded.

"Okay, then. Not a word."

Thank god she had the kind of relationship with her daughter that Deanne did what she was told.

Concealing themselves in that airless attic until the men left turned out to be an ordeal in self-control, but she managed it, squeezing herself and Deanne behind a stack of furniture in a corner. No one would ever know there was even an inch of room behind it. Keeping Deanne quiet was another miracle. She heard the sound of angry voices, two strangers shouting and banging things. Searching for all the artifacts, because Sutherland had tossed her to the wolves. If he were in front of her right now, she might kill him.

How on earth had he even gotten himself into this mess? Stupid question. After listening to him, she knew how. But what kind of poker game got him into this?

Voices drifted up again through the air ducts.

"We have to find something, anything," she heard one of the men say. "The boss had us search Sutherland's house even though he said he didn't have it, but he has no reason to tell the truth. Now he's in the wind. He told the boss the stuff was here, but who the fuck would trust him after this?"

"He never should have grabbed the whole shipment," the man with the deepest voice said. "If in fact that's what he did. He had a sweet deal going with Welborn, and now it's fucked. And he's saying this woman was the one who stole it? What the hell? Something smells bad here."

"You don't suppose he found another buyer and did a double cross, do you?"

"Double cross Welborn? That's an automatic death sentence. It's possible, but who would be stupid enough to get in the boss's crosshairs? I still say Sutherland has the whole shipment. If he can sell it off, he can hide away on some insignificant island with a new identity and be out of all this for the rest of his life. Maybe that's what the boss is so pissed about."

New identity? What on earth was Craig Sutherland involved in? How come in ten years she hadn't even heard a whisper about it? And who on earth was this boss? Could it be Roger Welborn?

"If he did, his brains are in his ass. There won't be a place on this earth he can hide."

"Yeah? Well, holy fuck. How stupid is that. What's he planning to do with it?"

"I guess he didn't realize the boss is so obsessed with this stuff he'll go to any lengths to retrieve."

"Are you kidding? When you've got as much

money as he does, you can afford to be obsessed with something. But we both know double crossing him is a sure trip to the cemetery."

"Well, Sutherland's obviously lied about the LaCroix woman having the stuff. There's nothing here. I didn't believe that the minute I heard it. Neither did the boss, but he said we had to check it out. Maybe grab her at the same time and shake whatever she knew out of her."

Nausea welled up in Jen's throat. She'd thought she knew Craig pretty well, but obviously not. Especially if he'd sacrifice her to save himself.

"Except she's not here and neither are the missing pieces," the man with the deeper voice pointed out. "Where the hell did that bitch disappear to, anyway? Did he point the finger at her, then warn her away?"

"That's the question of the day. She's not even answering her phone."

"Of course not," the other man snapped. "Would you? She's probably ditched it by now."

"If we can't find those pieces, we're royally fucked. The boss will not be happy about it, and you know how he gets when he's unhappy. I can't believe she got here and left already. We headed out here as soon as we got the call and that schmuck Sutherland said she was at the museum."

"I wouldn't put stock in anything he said," the man with the deeper voice commented.

"Whatever, but we need to find the woman," his friend told him. "That's what we need to do. And her kid. If we get the kid, that gives us leverage with her."

Oh, god. Deanne!

Jen looked at her daughter, huddled behind the

furniture with her.

"Yeah? Well, Mr. Brains, right now we can't find either of them or that expensive junk. Let's check all the rooms again. I'd bet my ass nothing's here, but I want to be able to tell the boss we covered every square inch."

Jen felt as if she was holding her breath while the sounds of the search echoed through the small cabin. When they looked in the attic, she held her breath, praying they couldn't spot her and Deanne behind the furniture. She was sure they were completely hidden but anything was possible. She barely allowed herself to breathe as she listened to the rage in their voices as they argued about the lack of results.

"There's nothing up here but a bunch of old junk covered with dust." This from the man who seemed to be in charge. "It's not here. I bet he called her before we got to him, and she ran with all the stuff. Maybe she's meeting him with it. Fuck it all. Let's get out of here and see if we can pick up a trail on the bitch and her daughter. She can't have gone far."

"What if we can't find them? Either the bitch and her kid or…" There was an edge of panic in this voice.

"Then we'd damn well better find a hiding place for ourselves, someplace the boss won't get to us. If there is such a place."

Jen heard heavy footsteps, then the front door to the house opening and closing. Her every instinct was to scramble out of their hiding place, but she forced herself to wait for what seemed an eternity. Time enough for them to get tired of looking. One hour. Two hours. The minute hand on her watch crept by with agonizing slowness, but she had to be sure the men were gone.

How had she gotten into this mess, anyway? She'd thought living in Michigan and working in a museum would be a nice safe existence. Craig Sutherland was smuggling antiquities right under everyone's nose and selling them to...to whom? God knew some of the wealthiest people in the Midwest lived in the area. It could be any one of them. The big question was how the thing started in the first place. Obviously Welborn, Mister Big Shot, was in an illegal scheme where he paid Sutherland to smuggle stolen items into the country for him. How had that started? And what did the card game have to do with it?

She tried to move as little as possible. Mercifully, Deanne had fallen asleep.

Finally, when it was dark, Jen crept out of the corner of the attic where they'd been hiding and slid open the almost invisible panel that led back to the floor below. She swung the rope ladder over the side and climbed down, dropped to the floor, and reached up for Deanne.

"I'm scared," the tiny voice said.

"Me, too, sweetheart. We'll be fine, though. I promise." Jennifer hugged her daughter. "But we need to get out of here."

"But where will we go?" Deanne's voice trembled as she asked the question.

Damn you, Craig Sutherland, for putting me and my daughter in this situation.

"Someplace you'll like." She hoped. "Okay?"

Slowly, Deanne nodded. Carrying their suitcases, they moved like smoky wraiths toward the trees, where her car was hidden. It took a while to pull off all the camouflage and ease out to the road. As she headed for the highway, she was as tense as she'd ever been. The fact it was raining didn't help things, but the gun in her console gave her confidence.

She was pretty sure she'd made a clean getaway for herself and her daughter from the house, undetected or so she hoped. Until a car shot out of a driveway and pulled up behind her. Was that them? Her question was answered when the truck banged her rear bumper, making the car jerk forward.

Ohgodohgodohgod.

She slammed her foot on the accelerator, and her car jerked forward. When she'd discovered the car she bought two years ago had a souped-up engine, she almost gave it back. Now, she was glad she hadn't as she managed to stay far enough ahead of the vehicle behind her. They were almost to the Interstate. Almost. Almost.

Please, please, please.

And there was an entrance. She cut off another vehicle, shoving her way onto the highway, and sliced across two lanes of traffic. She drove as fast as she could, weaving in and out of traffic, checking the rearview mirror, until she was sure she was far enough ahead of the chase car. Back across three lanes of traffic to an exit ramp.

The vehicle behind her didn't quite make the exit, but she had to make sure she'd lost them. So back onto the Interstate and two more on-and-off into busy intersections before she finally believed it was safe to move forward. Gripping the steering wheel with both hands she focused on the road ahead, glancing every few moments in her rearview mirror. Was that the car behind her following her? Waiting for the next opportunity? Were any of them?

At another exit, she pulled off, turned into a gas station to top off the tank, and ditched her cell. She was nervous about the long drive ahead without a phone, but she didn't want anything that would tell someone where she was or where she was going. She was a total wreck by the time they hit the Interstate headed south and knew she needed to pull herself together. For Deanne if not for herself. She could sense the fear coming from her child, a feeling she shared but had to conceal.

The rain grew heavier and steadier. The roads were slick even on the superhighways, and cars driving too fast fishtailed, sending up great rooster tails of water that splashed the windshield of the car. She looked in the rearview mirror constantly, straining to see any movement in the blackness behind her.

What a mess this whole thing was. It couldn't be much worse. Her job was on hold, the FBI wanted to talk to her, and Craig Sutherland had skewered her head on a pike.

She was lucky she'd gotten away, but she needed to clamp down on the fear before she ran her car off the road. She took every evasive precaution that she'd learned in her life long ago, on and off the interstate. Exiting the Interstate, driving through small towns and up and down side streets, pulling into large, crowded parking lots like grocery stores, and watching to see what cars came and went. Then back onto the Interstate heading south as fast as the speed limit would let her.

Damn.

All she'd wanted was a nice quiet life for herself and Deanne. Instead, she'd ended up in a big mess with her job and maybe her life on the line. A situation that was finally going to connect Deanne with the father she'd kept hidden from her all these years. Maybe this was her punishment for not contacting Dino a long time ago.

Now, she was headed for the only place she knew would be safe, a place where she could leave Deanne and then get away from everyone.

Dino will find out about Deanne.

And whose fault was it that it hadn't happened before now. Well, it just couldn't be helped, and she had no idea at all what his reaction would be. When he found out the truth, would he be pissed off? Angry he'd been denied all these years? What if she told him she loved him but had been afraid to tell him? Would he think she was stupid because she fell for him, or had he been hiding his own feelings?

God. The more the questions tumbled around inside her, the more her stomach hurt. If she could just leave Deanne with the Caines and disappear, but she knew that wouldn't work. Dino would look for her, especially once he saw Deanne. That was just who he was. At least, for the moment, her daughter would be safe with Ethan, and she'd have breathing space to figure out what to say to Dino when the time came.

Because it would. She couldn't just park Deanne there forever.

She hoped she still remembered where she was going. Dino had taken her there once, in another lifetime. Maybe she'd been too hasty running away from him, not giving him a chance to decide about the unplanned pregnancy. But he'd made sure everyone knew he wasn't a man who wanted obligations. That his lifestyle didn't work with them. She hadn't wanted to be an obligation that he'd resent.

She prayed Ethan would agree to what she asked, knowing at the same time he'd tell Dino what was going on. Because one look at this little girl and there was no denying who her father was. There'd probably be hell to pay if this ever all got straightened out, but she'd cross that bridge when she came to it.

Thankfully, Deanne, whether from shock or exhaustion, had fallen asleep as soon as they hit the Interstate. She'd slept off and on, waking when they stopped for food at a drive-through, eating in the car in a dark corner of the lot. Jen needed the coffee more than anything. The hamburger she'd eaten still sat like a lump of lead in her stomach. But Deanne needed food.

It was a long drive from Michigan to Florida, but she pushed it as far as she could. At least her hands had finally stopped shaking. When she absolutely couldn't keep her eyes open any longer, she pulled off into a small town, found a cheap motel where she didn't think anyone would look for her, and crashed.

Deanne was grumpy and whiny, not unexpected, and she had to spend some time calming her down, trying to explain where they were going and why, without scaring the pants off her. Breakfast settled her down again before they got back on the road, although much later than Jen had hoped. She spent valuable time popping on and off the Interstate, driving through the outskirts of little towns before she felt sure no one had located them. Still, every car that drew too close to her or cut in front of her made her stomach knot and panic rise in her throat.

She'd racked her brain for the best solution. She

herself had to disappear. Since that jackass Sutherland had connected her name to the missing artifacts everyone from the FBI to the moneyman was looking for her. This was her best alternative, a safe place for Deanne while she disappeared from sight until this terrible mess went away.

Deanne. That's the only thing that had been on her mind. Safety for her daughter. And help getting these people off her back. Ethan Caine could provide the first. She considered calling Dino, but...

Don't go there. That could be a disaster. You have no idea what his reaction would be after all this time and the way you ran away from him, never even giving him a chance.

Ran away was pretty accurate. But at the time she hadn't known how her secret would offend him or anger him. It had been better not to know, especially since she'd had to work hard to conceal her feelings for him.

Ethan would do what she needed while she disappeared. If there was one thing she knew, it was that he could be trusted to protect her daughter.

After a long silence, Deanne asked, "Where are we going?"

Jen reached over and squeezed her hand. "To someone I know who can help us, sweetheart. A man who can make this all right."

"Is that man my dad?" Deanne asked the question in a soft, tentative voice.

Jen wondered what everyone would say when the truth came out. What Dino would say.

"No, sweetheart, but when this is all over, I will make sure you meet him."

If he'll even talk to me.

What with all the detours and evasive maneuvers she continued to take and a quick stop of a drive-through dinner, it was early evening before they reached their destination. She couldn't believe she actually remembered where the house was. Except it was very different. Last time she'd seen it, the place had been surrounded by overgrown prairie grass and weeds and the paint had been visibly peeling. Through the spokes of a wrought iron gate, she could see the long drive to the house was paved and the grass had been cut down. A high wall surrounded the property, with a speaker box jutting out next to the gate.

Wow, Ethan. You must have made some pretty big changes in your life.

She pulled up to the gate, rolled down her window, and stuck her arm out in the pelting rain to press the button on the speaker box.

"Yes? Who is this?" The still familiar voice crackled in the storm-charged air.

"Ethan? Ethan, it's me. Jennifer. Jen LaCroix." What if he didn't remember her?

"Jen?" Even through the rain and static she could hear the shock in his voice.

If you think you're shocked now, wait until you hear what I have to tell you.

"Yes. Can you open the gate and let us in?"

A brief pause. "Us? Who's with you?"

"No one who means you any harm," she told him impatiently. "Can you just open the gate? I'm getting soaked with the window open here."

"What is it? What do you want?"

"I need to see you." She gritted her teeth, listening

24

to Deanne stir in the back seat. "I know it's been a long time, but I wouldn't be here if it wasn't an emergency. Please, can we come in?"

Another pause. "All right. Come on ahead."

The gate swung open. Jen rolled up the window and drove slowly up to the big, rambling farmhouse. The front porch lights had come on as soon as the gate opened, and Ethan Caine stood framed in the doorway. But as she drew up to the front steps, even through the rain, she could see it was a different Ethan Caine than she'd expected.

Like the house and the land, he'd undergone a transformation. His beard was trimmed, and his hair was drawn back into a neat ponytail. He'd lost a good bit of weight, and where once there had been burgeoning fat and softness, now beneath the T-shirt and jeans, she saw a hard muscular body. What the hell had happened to him?

The only thing familiar to her was the gun he held at his side.

"Mom?" Deanne had released her seat belt and slid over next to Jen. "Why does that man have a gun? Is he going to shoot someone, too?"

"No, honey. It's okay." She hoped.

A slender, dark-haired woman appeared behind Ethan, shoving an umbrella into his free hand and giving him a little push.

Aha! Even the wildest of the wild can be tamed, apparently.

Ethan opened the umbrella and came down to the car, walking around to the driver's side. "Hello, Jen."

"Please put the gun away," she told him. "You're scaring Deanne."

Shoving the gun in his pants at the small of his back, he pulled his shirt loose to cover it. He peered past her into the darkness, checking for any other movement, making sure no one had breached the security behind her.

"We're alone," she assured him. "Listen, can we please come inside? It's soaking wet outside, and Deanne is freezing."

His eyes narrowed as he took in the child plastered to her side. "Yours?"

"Of course," she snapped. "And she's exhausted. Are you going to let us in?"

Ethan waited for the space of one more heartbeat, then called out, "All clear." To Jen and Deanne he said, "Come on."

He held the umbrella as they both slid out of the car and moved under it as best they could. They made a soggy bunch as they hurried up the steps to the porch.

The dark-haired woman gave them a warm smile and held out her hands in a welcoming gesture. "Hello. I'm Lisa Caine."

In a toneless voice, Ethan said, "Lisa, this is Jennifer LaCroix. And her daughter, Deanne. She knew Dino and I a long time ago."

"Come in. You're soaked, and I'm sure you're exhausted." Her glance at Ethan was an I'll-talk-to-you-about-this later look.

"I'm sorry to barge in on you like this," Jen apologized, teeth chattering, "but I just didn't know where else to go." She tightened her arm around the little girl who looked at Ethan with frightened eyes.

A young boy around ten years old materialized in the hallway, stationing himself close to Ethan.

"Everything okay, Dad?"

Dad?

"Everything's fine." Ethan raked his eyes over the pair in front of him. "Well, Jen. What's going on?"

Lisa made a disgusted sound in her throat. "Ethan, for God's sake. They'll catch pneumonia if you leave them standing there like this." She smiled at Jen. "Please let me help you into some dry clothes and get you something hot to drink."

"We have clothes in the car," Jen protested. "I can just dash out—"

"Absolutely not. Tomorrow will be time enough. I think I can outfit the two of you just fine for now."

"T-That would be wonderful. Thank you. I apologize—"

Lisa waved a hand at her. "Later." She smiled at the boy. "This is our son, Jamie. Honey, go to your room and get a pair of jeans and a T-shirt from the pile of last year's clothes we just cleaned out." She gave Jennifer an assessing look. "I think you and I are about the same size. We can make do."

Deanne held tight to Jen's hand as they followed Lisa down a short hallway to one of the guest bedrooms.

"I think a hot shower would do you both good," Lisa told her. "By the time you're finished, I'll have something laid out on the bed for you both."

"But you don't even know anything about us," Jennifer protested. "How can you be so calm with two complete strangers? Doesn't Ethan...I mean, hasn't Ethan..."

Lisa smiled. "Ethan said you knew each other a long time ago. He let you in the house and didn't shoot you. That's good enough for me."

"This is really an awkward situation," Jen blurted out, stroking Deanne's damp hair. "I didn't expect…I don't know what I expected."

"Well," Lisa grinned, "unless you're here trying to steal my husband, it doesn't matter."

"Nothing like that." Jen let out the breath she'd been holding. "We really need Ethan's help with something. We're in big trouble."

"I know he'll do anything if he can. Hot shower, then a hot drink. Do you prefer coffee or tea?"

"Tea with a little brandy, if that's all right."

"No problem."

They showered quickly, then Jen dried them both off and grabbed the clothes Lisa had left for them on the bed. Seeing Ethan, married with a son and his act cleaned up, made her wonder if Dino had done the same thing. If so, then she was really screwed, because she was hoping Ethan would contact him and tell him about Deanne. That was her focus. Her daughter. Their daughter. Well, she'd find out soon enough and then figure out what came next.

They were just walking into the kitchen when she heard Ethan's voice, low and indistinguishable.

Then Lisa asked, "Really? I wonder how she found you. Could she have contacted someone you're working with now? Would she even know who to call?"

"Since Ethan apparently hasn't mentioned it," Jen said as they walked into the kitchen, "I was here a few times years ago with Dino Brancuzzi. Ethan, do you remember that?"

Ethan and Lisa both turned at the sound of her voice, wearing identical startled looks.

"Sorry." Jen cleared her throat. "I didn't mean to eavesdrop. Anyway, I guess my brain just remembered how to get here." She looked around the room. "I must say the place bears little resemblance to what I saw then. I guess you get the congrats for that, Lisa."

"Actually, it was a joint operation." Lisa looked at Ethan and smiled. "We work well together."

This is an extraordinary woman. I could never handle this the way she is.

"Thanks for the clothes, by the way." She felt uncomfortable about it, but the woman was so gracious she could hardly make an issue of it.

"Well, the outfits won't make a fashion statement"—Lisa grinned—"but at least they aren't soaking wet. In the morning, we'll get your stuff out of your car. I made some hot tea and spiked it with Ethan's best brandy. And I've got hot chocolate for…Deanne, is it?"

"Yes." Jen hugged her daughter close. "Sweetie, I have to talk privately with Mr. Caine and his wife. Okay?" She looked at Ethan. "Would it be possible for your son to find something to occupy Deanne for a while? Maybe a video game or something? She's pretty good at them, even at her age."

Ethan and Lisa looked at their son, a signal passing among them.

Jamie had obviously learned his cues a long time ago. He pushed back his chair and stood up. "Sure. Come on," he said to Deanne. "You like video games? I've got some cool ones I can show you."

"No, Mom." Deanne pushed herself even closer to her mother's body. "I want to stay in here with you. Please." She clung as if her life depended on it.

Jen disengaged her arms and kissed her forehead. "It will be all right, honey. Nothing bad is going to happen here. I promise. I told you when I decided to come here that Mr. Caine could protect us, and he will. I just have to talk to him and tell him what happened, okay?"

"But—"

"No buts. Go with Jamie. Let us talk, and then I'll tell you exactly what's going on. Okay? Can you trust me on this?"

After her daughter left the room, Jen dropped into a chair at the table, not sure how much longer her legs would hold her, and took a grateful sip from the cup Lisa set in front of her.

"Protect you?" Ethan casually took a swallow of his coffee from the mug he was holding. "Protect you from what?"

Oh, God. Where do I start?

Jennifer sighed. "It's a long story, and not a very pleasant one, I'm afraid. For a lot of reasons I didn't want to reach out to Dino, the biggest being I wasn't sure if he'd just hang up the phone on me. I need help, and I didn't know who else to reach out to."

"No offense intended, Jen, but with you, I wouldn't expect any different."

"Ethan!" Lisa's voice had a scolding edge to it. "My God, let the woman tell us what's going on before you start throwing barbs at her."

Jen fiddled with her cup. "It's all right. Ethan, I know how you feel about me. But Deanne and I are in big, big trouble. I thought about contacting Dino, but I was afraid he'd think I was lying to him about Deanne just to get protection for her. She needs to be somewhere safe while I figure a way out of this mess. Besides, after the way I left all those years ago, I'm sure he's not anxious to have anything to do with me."

"Okay, what's the deal?"

She told him as briefly but completely as she could what had happened, and Ethan listened without interrupting her.

"So that's it." She leaned back in her chair, emotionally drained. "The FBI is already all over it. Craig Sutherland has apparently dumped it all on me. I could see I was about to be the scapegoat, and I don't want to end up in prison just because they think I'm guilty and an easy scapegoat. I grabbed Deanne and got the hell out of there. I've got to make myself invisible until the truth comes out."

"No doubt. And yes, I can help you. I can tell when someone's lying to me, and my bullshit meter isn't registering anything." He narrowed his eyes. "But why bother Dino at all? It isn't as if you just saw each other yesterday. And you're probably right. If I recall, he was damn pissed with the way you disappeared on him."

Jennifer picked up her spoon and slowly stirred sugar into the brandy-laced tea, her eyes on the dark liquid while she tried to figure out how he was going to react to her news. Her heart hammered against her ribs, and all her breath felt trapped in her throat. She was about to play her trump card, and she had no idea what would happen when she did. "Because he's the only one who'd have a vested interest in doing so."

"Yeah? And exactly why is that?"

She looked at him, her gaze holding his, aware of Lisa watching both of them with curiosity. "Because Deanne is his daughter."

31

Chapter Three

Key West, Florida

The night was black and moonless, just the way Dino Brancuzzi liked it. And since running without lights was a common event for him, he had no problem guiding his boat in total darkness. The boat bumped quietly against the piles as he slowly eased it into position and cut the engine.

Leaping soundlessly to the dock, he tied off the lines on his boat. The only light came from the few dim lampposts that lit the pier. He scanned the area carefully, checking the surrounding boats, looking for signs of activity. Nothing and no one seemed to be moving. At this hour of the night—or morning, as it actually was—he didn't expect anything to happen, but he never let down his guard. That led to disaster.

Everything appeared normal so he reached into his pocket, pulled out a small remote, and clicked it. One click, and the pier lights were extinguished. They'd have to hurry. Who knew how long they had before some tenant popped out to gripe about there being trouble with the lighting again?

He whistled softly, then dropped the ladder and climbed down to the pier. The door to the cabin opened and three men appeared, also dressed in black. Two of the men silently negotiated the ladder to join Dino on the pier. Then they both reached out to help the third man make his descent. He moved slowly, obviously injured and favoring one side of his body, but soon they were all heading noiselessly along the pier in the darkness.

They moved as quickly as possible to the parking lot separated from the pier by a chain link fence. Minutes later Dino, watched as the two men climbed into a black SUV, ready to head away from the marina. The man in the driver's seat rolled down his window a scant two inches.

"Good job, as always," he told Dino. "Thanks."

Dino nodded. "Take care of your friend there."

"Will do. You'll be hearing from me again."

Dino grinned. "I'm counting on it."

The SUV pulled out of the lot and made a left onto the highway before turning on its lights. When he was sure they were safely away, he turned on the pier lights again.

The trip back from the extraction zone had taken longer than he'd expected. Especially when they'd had to run without lights in certain parts of the Gulf. But it had all been worth it. Even the tiny nick in his arm from a bullet that came too close. In a week, he'd be healed, adding one more scar to his growing collection.

Heading back through the gate, he began a slow walk down the pier. Although he was a big man, he'd learned over the years, first in the CIA, then in the service and as a private contractor for Guardian Security and now running Blackwater, to move almost soundlessly and with an economy of motion. He always dressed in black, knowing other colors reflected the light, and his hair was pulled taut in its usual ponytail to avoid getting in his way. Tonight, he'd also covered his face with black camouflage so nothing would give him away.

Dino always liked to check everything before he locked up for the night, a habit long-ingrained in him. He'd bought the marina when he couldn't decide what to do with himself. He was alone in the world. His parents had been killed in an automobile accident, and he'd managed to run the only woman he really loved out of his life. The government came calling with a request for an op, and after that, another and then another, until it became a regular thing.

He'd owned the marina for a long time now, and every inch of it was burned into his brain, as familiar as his own bed. One day, after a couple of years, just as he was getting ready to go out, a couple of tourists stranded on the dock asked if he'd take them out for the afternoon, and Blackwater Charters was born.

He rented out several of the slips to others on a more or less permanent basis. Along with the fishing charters he took on now and then, it provided a nice cover for his operation and gave Blackwater Charters a higher level of legitimacy. Add in the work he did off and on for Guardian Security, and he thought he had a good life. No obligations, nothing defining his life except himself. When memories of Jen intruded into his brain, he shut them down, unwilling to keep looking at his stupidity.

The snick of a sliding door opening caused him to swivel to the right. A man appeared on one of the boats, climbing up onto the deck.

"Hey, Dino," he called. "You'd better get those lights fixed. They keep conking out."

"It's just a glitch in the wiring," Dino called back. "Anyway," he joked, "for what you're doing, you shouldn't want any light."

The man laughed and disappeared back inside his boat.

Dino retraced his steps to his office at the shoreside end of the pier. Blackwater Charters was housed in what looked like little more than a shack at the head of the pier. But anyone trying to break in would set off multiple alarms—set to protect the inside—which would have been the envy of any technophile. High performance computers and communications gear lined two walls, securely bolted to shelves. A row of satellite phones sat in a rack next to his desk.

To the left of his desk, inside open cupboard doors, were a row of monitors hooked up to a state-of-the art security system. Those doors could be closed and locked when the wrong eyes might see them. It wasn't so much the fishing business Blackwater did that required such a sophisticated electronic setup as the "black" work they did that more than fit their name.

The people who chartered him for deep sea fishing were completely unaware of the real nature of Blackwater.

He checked the monitors to make sure everything in the parking area as well as the pier was secure. No strangers hanging around. No one who might have hidden and seen his passenger disembark. In the small bathroom off the office, he pulled a bottle of aspirin out of the medicine cabinet, shook three into his hand, and swallowed them dry.

Catching sight of himself in the mirror, he shook his head. Not bad for forty-two. Except for the recent bullet scrape and some well-worn scars, he kept himself in excellent physical shape. Looking closely, he spotted a few more gray hairs in the ponytail and a few more lines around his eyes. But he was still at the top of his game.

It seemed like just yesterday he'd been holding his shiny new diploma when a man in a black suit approached him with an offer that changed the course of his life. It wasn't until he arrived at Langley, Virginia for intense training that he realized just how much of a change and what was expected of him.

He had special skills they were looking for, like the ability to blend in with any crowd or community. An aptitude with languages. A quick mind and an extraordinary ability to think on his feet. No desk job for Nina and Tito Brancuzzi's little boy. Before he could finish telling his parents his cover story, he was whisked away into the shadowy world of spy and counterspy, doing whatever was asked of him and doing it so well he surprised even himself.

Along the way, he collected two things—a raft of enemies and a friendship with Ethan Caine. Of all the people he knew in the world, there was no one he trusted more. They met during a joint operation when Ethan was working for another one of the alphabet agencies and hung together whenever possible. It always amazed him how many times their paths crossed as they went about their jobs.

He'd always wanted a boat, so after a particularly dangerous mission, he figured Fate was sending him a sign. He landed in Key West with all the money he'd stashed away over the years, eventually bought the house and the marina and settled back to spend his days on the water, fishing, and sometimes diving, a new hobby. Until the day those tourists had asked for a trip and Blackwater was born. Then Langley came calling, after years of no contact, and asked if he'd take a fishing charter of a different kind, and a new pattern was set.

Leaning back in his chair, he tried to decide if he wanted to head out for a well-deserved drink at a bar or go home and flop down on the couch and drink his own liquor. There was no one waiting for him there. His last relationship, like all the others, ended when his friend decided she wanted to make the sleepovers permanent, and Dino ran like a scalded ass ape.

His one long-term relationship had ended badly, probably his fault, but images of Jennifer LaCroix still filled his dreams more often than he liked. You'd think, after ten years, he'd finally get her out of his mind, but no, Fate or whatever persisted in tormenting him. Dreaming about her luscious curves, her full breasts with their rosy nipples, and the small, trimmed patch of auburn hair that decorated her mound were enough to make his cock harden and beg for release. At times like that, he was grateful for the strength of his good right hand. Getting himself off wasn't nearly as good as plunging his dick into Jennifer's heat, but it was sure less complicated.

But it wasn't just the sex. She had a laugh that filled him with joy, a zest for life, a way about her that brought sunshine into every room. His determination to remain untethered, independent—whatever the fuck that was— had been the root cause of the end of his relationship with Jen. Not that she said anything to him. In fact, she said nothing, just up and left when he was off on a trip. It shocked him how much he missed her and how long it took him to get over it. Even now, he always felt as if a piece of him was missing.

My own damn fault. Ethan walked away with the prize, and all I have are regrets.

He had felt only minor pangs of envy when his old friend, Ethan, married Lisa Mallory. He smiled, thinking about the mission Ethan had undertaken for Lisa two years ago, one that Dino and Blackwater had been a major part of. What a rescue and extraction that job had been, plucking Lisa's son away from drug dealers in the middle of the Mexican jungle. Now, the man was unbelievably settled into domestic life.

Once upon a time, Dino had wanted the same things Ethan had now. Too bad he didn't actually know it or realize it until the only woman he'd wanted them with slipped away. His own damn fucking fault. Too busy being the king of dark assignments to pay attention to what was right under his nose. And he'd regretted it every single day since then. For ten years now, he'd felt as if a big piece of his life was missing. Which it was.

When Ethan had given up the old life after a disastrous assignment, he'd isolated himself at the family farm he inherited and done his best to drink himself to death. But Lisa had changed all that. Ethan had settled easily into family life, surprising everyone who knew him, both as a covert government agent and mercenary. He cleaned up his act and put his skills to use doing contract work for Guardian Security and running a school for mercenaries and corporate security teams. In fact, Ethan was the one who brought him on board with the agency his friend had worked for before returning to black ops for a while.

The huge barn sitting about an acre behind Ethan's house had been rehabbed and turned into classrooms, an electronics center, and a huge gym. There was also a knockdown house for hostage rescue training and a state-of-the-art gun range. Dino also knew that Ethan still consulted in certain situations but tried to keep those to a minimum. He was mostly out of the life now.

And exceedingly happy.

Dino wondered more and more what it would be like to have someone like Lisa in his life. And every time he did, Jennifer had popped into his dreams. Each time, though, he laughed at himself. The same old excuses applied now as then. He lived too much on the edge of danger and was too much of an adrenaline junkie to deal with a wife. He always managed to push those thoughts to the back of his mind.

Except for times like now.

It killed him to realize how he'd fucked up the best thing that ever happened to him. God. If only he could turn back the clock. Or somehow have her back in his life again.

He leaned back in his chair and closed his eyes, figuring he'd rest a little and then head home. These "projects" were taking more and more out of him. But the chair he was in was not the place to catch a nap. Just leaning back in it, he felt as if he was lying on a board. Heaving a sigh, he checked his answering machine for fishing charter bookings. They paid him a nice living in between his black ops jobs and gave him the semblance of a regular life. He was rummaging through a drawer for a pencil to make notes when his private satellite phone rang.

"Yes?" He never gave his name when he answered until he knew who was at the other end.

"You up for a little trip, buddy?" Ethan's voice rumbled across the connection. Speak of the devil.

Dino dropped into the chair. "I don't know. The last time you called me for a favor, I ended up running through the Quintana Roo jungle in Mexico with an AK-47 under my arm and a scared kid over my shoulder."

"And that scared kid is now my son and happy and healthy. No, this is a little different. This is just a little private plane ride."

"Depends where. You offering me an all-expense paid vacation with a bevy of naked broads?"

"Please." Ethan laughed, although Dino heard the edge of strain in it. "I'm a respectable family man now. I don't deal in such debauchery."

"Yeah, yeah, yeah." Dino propped his feet on the desk. "So, to what do I really owe the honor of this call at—" He looked at his watch. "—almost one in the morning."

"I hope you're sitting down."

"Lay it on me, Ethan. There isn't much you can say that would shock me."

"Oh yeah? Wait until you hear this."

"Hear what?" Dino asked.

"Lisa and I had an unexpected visitor tonight." He paused for effect. "Jen LaCroix."

Dino's breath froze. Jen? Jen showed up at Ethan's out of the blue? How? Why? So many memories suddenly assaulted him he had to force himself to take a deep breath. Jennifer LaCroix was the only woman he'd ever thought about giving a permanent place in his life.

But he'd been too chickenshit to do it and then she was gone. Disappeared.

Was this Fate giving him another chance? He swallowed and forced himself to take a deep breath.

"Why was she there?" he finally managed to ask. "What did she want?"

"It seems she's in some trouble at the place where she's been working, and she was looking for help and a safe haven. I guess I was the first one she thought of."

Dino clenched his jaw. "Not me?"

Pause.

"I'm sure she thought disappearing the way she did might have pissed you off. She wanted someone who could provide safety and not be angry with her."

What? The? Fuck?

"What kind of trouble?"

"If you've got a way to get your ass up here, I'll tell you all about it, and maybe get her to answer some questions for you."

"And Dino? It seems you have a daughter. A cute little girl named Deanne."

Dino felt shock race through him like an electric bolt. Holy shit! He used all his discipline to pull himself together.

"I'm on my way," he told his friend and finally clicked off, still in shock.

He closed his eyes, rubbing his fingers across his forehead to ease the tension. He still had trouble believing the conversation. A daughter. He had a daughter. One he'd never known about. Talk about a shocker. Holy shit! And Jen! He could just imagine Ethan's reaction when she and her child showed up on his doorstep, scared to death about something.

God! He counted backwards and realized she'd had to be pregnant the last time they were together. So why hadn't she told him about it?

Because you're such a selfish dick, and she knew you'd react badly.

A flat truth that actually hurt him to accept.

He'd been all about no strings, no attachments, and the high that came from the covert work he did. The words "settling down" weren't even in his vocabulary, and he'd hadn't been shy letting people know about it.

No wonder she didn't tell you, asshole.

He'd never thought about having kids. He was still dealing with the shock of Ethan's marriage to Lisa and him adopting her son. He'd never seen him as a family man, but that was exactly what he'd become and apparently, thrived in that role.

Now he was facing a similar but different situation, and what the fuck was he supposed to do?

On one hand, he was relieved he'd never had to worry about a kid all these years while he was pushing the envelope. On the other, he was pissed as hell she'd never told him. Ethan had asked if he wanted to talk to her, and his first reaction was to say no. What the hell would he say to her? And she was running from something. Ethan didn't have the story yet, but so what? What was he supposed to do?

His lifestyle certainly wasn't conducive to family living, and besides, there was no telling what kind of trouble she'd gotten herself into. Ten years had passed since the last time he'd seen her. She'd partied with his wild crowd, looked for the edge in every situation, and burned the sheets in his bed with the hottest sex he'd ever had. If there were ten different ways to fuck,

Jennifer explored them all. Reckless and independent were two words he'd always used to describe her. Oh. And hot. Yes. Indeed. Fucking hot.

And god, wasn't that just the truth. With Jen, he had the best sex ever. She was hot and unrestrained, giving one hundred percent. Some nights, the dreams he had of them together made him so aroused only a cold shower and his good right hand could give him any sleep. If he even thought of the heat of her wrapped around his throbbing shaft, he was instantly and painfully hard.

It wasn't just sex, either. She was smart and funny and easy to be with. So why in the holy fuck hadn't he figured out a way to keep them together? Or realized what he actually had? Was he so afraid of restrictions on his life, so busy being Mr. Macho, that he let the best woman he'd ever met walk out of it?

Yes, you dumbass, and you've paid for it ever since.

He had few regrets in his life, but this was definitely at the top of the list. He'd done his best to write her out of his memory, but he'd never been able to do it. He could close his eyes at night and still remember the feel of his cock sliding into the hot channel of her sex, slick with her liquids. Her breasts pressed against his chest, the rosy tips hard and firm. Her inner walls gripping him and milking his cock until he didn't have a drop left to give.

Well, hell. That wasn't helping.

What was her story now? First, he had to learn that, and that meant talking to her and getting some answers. And asking her why Ethan had called and not her. Maybe he didn't want to know that answer, but he was fucking well going to find out.

Knowing he'd never sleep after Ethan's call, he adjusted the office chair as best he could and leaned back, hoping to catch at least a few minutes of sleep. He did manage to doze off but kept waking up when images of Jen filled his head, tormenting him.

At seven o'clock he was unable to wait any longer. Sighing, knowing that he was stepping into a big tar pit, he picked up the phone and dialed a familiar number.

Mike Hogan was part of the regular team Dino used for contract work and someone he trusted implicitly. The owner of Key West Charters, the man provided chopper services whenever it was required, like now.

"This is kind of early for you," Mike said as he answered the phone.

"Crank up the Beechcraft. We're invited to breakfast."

"What the hell? What's going on? Why can't I use the chopper?"

"I'll tell you when I see you. Be there shortly."

Dino spotted Mike finishing his preflight on his helicopter when he pulled into the air charter service lot. He parked his car and walked over to shake hands with his friend.

"I assume you'll tell me what this is all about when we're in the air?" Mike said.

"I'm not sure I even believe it myself, but Ethan called and said to get my ass up there now."

"You're the boss." Mike stowed his clipboard. "Okay. Let's do it."

They swung out over the Gulf of Mexico and hugged its coastline, the sun a yellow ball on their right moving higher in the sky. Dino gave Mike the abbreviated version of his very short call with Ethan Caine. Then he slipped on his aviator shades and tilted his head back against the seat.

"Wake me when we get there," he said over the headset.

So much was swirling around in his brain he had to work at staying calm. He needed to at least appear in control when he met his daughter for the first time.

His daughter! God! He just hoped he handled things well when he met her.

There was surprisingly little air traffic on the trip up from Key West. It seemed as if only seconds had passed when Mike tapped his arm and pointed down. Below them was the Caine farmland, acres of wild grasses except for the area around the house and the newly built training facility. And running down the middle, a wide black strip that was the runway. Looking down through the window, he saw the back door of the house open and Ethan, in jeans and T-shirt, walk toward the end of the runway.

He hadn't seen his friend for some time, although they kept in touch electronically. He realized the man looked damn good. He'd gotten himself in shape when he went to Mexico to rescue Jamie, and apparently, he'd kept it up. He was a little older but still lean and mean and tough.

"I hope that breakfast is damned good." Dino shook hands with Ethan.

"No kidding." Mike took his turn with the greetings. "I had to throw a hot body out of my bed to haul this guy's ass up here."

"Okay, what the fuck is the story?" Dino asked his

friend. "I have a kid? For real? And Jen just showed up with her out of nowhere? I want to see both of them right now."

"Hold on." Ethan held up a hand. "There's a few things to get straight first."

"Like what?"

"Like the fact that Jen came here because she's more concerned about her daughter's safety—your daughter's—than anything else. But there's a problem."

Dino quirked a brow. "Worse than it already is?"

"Let's go inside and let me explain. But first you should know that Jen took off."

Dino stopped as if his feet had grown into the ground. "She took off? As in left?"

Could this possibly get any worse?

Ethan nodded. "Jen always was able to memorize things. She must have watched me punch the code to close the gate when she got here, because this morning, she opened it and drove away."

"Drove away?" Dino had a hard time holding onto his temper. "She managed to get away from the great Ethan Caine?"

"Don't rub it in," he griped. "Lisa already beat you to it. And yes, right under my nose. But she left a note."

"Oh, great. Fantastic. Where the fuck is it?"

"I've got it, but let's go inside before I give it to you. You'll need a lot of coffee for this one."

"Wait. Where's the kid?"

Ethan sighed. "Here. With us. And quit referring to her as the kid. She's your flesh and blood."

But calling her that kept his emotional armor on place in case this was a disaster.

Dino stared at him. "She left her? Just left her?

Here? What the hell?"

"It's all in the note. Come on."

"Fine. Lead the way." He was still trying to control his anger, although he wasn't sure who he was angry at, Jen or himself. And the mixture of emotions flooding him knocked him off balance. "Let's see what the fuck she's gotten herself into."

"You might want to put a lid on the curse words." Ethan's voice was tinged with humor. "I have a son, you know, with big ears. Not to mention your daughter who is with him."

"Fuck." He chuffed the word.

"Yeah, good job," Ethan laughed.

As they walked toward the house, Dino looked at the new buildings and the marksmanship and exercise courses that had been created.

"You've got quite a setup here," Mike commented.

"You should see what it used to look like." Dino snorted. "You would have suggested he get machines and knock it to the ground."

"You should come to visit more than once every five years and you'd see what's happening. Now come on. Lisa's got breakfast cooking."

The inside of the house also looked considerably different than the last time he'd seen it. The old farmhouse had undergone quite a facelift, due, he was sure, to Lisa's efforts.

He'd never thought Ethan Caine would turn into a domesticated individual and clean up his act. Apparently, however, when you fell in love your life could change in an instant.

Love!

Hell! The very word made him shudder. And

maybe that had been his problem.

Lisa was standing at the stove, but as soon as they walked in, Dino went to her and squeezed her in a bear hug.

"Hey, hey, hey," Ethan said. "That's my wife you're mauling."

"And who better to do it than us," Mike wisecracked, but he settled for a chaste kiss on the cheek.

"Jamie has Deanne in the game room," she told them, "but voices carry so try to keep the language PG, please."

"You talking to me?" Dino pretended to be shocked. "I'm always PG."

Ethan actually barked a laugh, and even Lisa giggled. It was what they all needed to break through the tension thick in the air.

"Can I see her?" Dino asked. "I want to actually see her."

"As soon as we all settle down," Ethan told him. "She's been through enough trauma, and I don't want to frighten her. I'll get them both in here shortly, but I want to give you the background first."

Dino didn't like it, but he also knew Ethan was right. He wanted to know what the fuck was going on. He still felt as if a tank had rolled over him. He wanted to see his daughter but not before he had some answers.

"Go on," Lisa told him. "Sit down."

She filled mugs with coffee and set them on the table.

"Where's the note?" he demanded.

"Sit," Ethan told him. "Swallow some coffee, and I'll give it to you."

Chapter Four

The coffee tasted like acid, but Dino dutifully fortified himself, then opened the folded sheet of paper Lisa handed to him. As he read it, he thought about asking Ethan to add a shot of bourbon to the cup. He had a feeling he might need it.

Dino,

This is kind of a long letter, but I hope you will read it all.

I know you must be shocked that I am reaching out to you after all this time, but you are the only person I could turn to. I had no way to contact you, which is how I ended up at Ethan's. With Deanne. Your daughter. Dino, she is such a lovely, bright little girl. You would just fall in love with her. I thought so many times about trying to find you when she was born, but I didn't want to intrude on your life, which I knew was one without tie downs.

When I discovered I was pregnant, I knew I had to find a way to settle down and make a home to raise my—our—daughter. Michigan was as far away as I could get. I managed to get a job working in a museum in the Detroit area and found a place for Deanne and I to live in a nice, rural, suburban area. I was able to build a nice life for us. Sort of. But my job was good, and I made decent money. Until it all fell apart.

I think, from what I overheard, my boss, Craig

Sutherland, director of the museum, has been using legitimate shipments of artifacts to the museum to smuggle items himself. Apparently, he's doing it for Roger Welborn, chairman of the museum's board of directors and disgustingly rich. Most of the shipments come from South America and travel up through the Caribbean. I don't know how he got started or why, only that the last museum shipment is missing, all of it. The shipping company swears he signed for it, but he's trying to throw the blame on me.

Now, he's disappeared, all the pieces are missing, and everyone from the museum board to Welborn to the FBI is looking for him…and me. I overheard him on the phone with Welborn, or I'd never even have an inkling of what was going on. Or that he's had something going for a long time at some high stakes private poker game he got invited to, and he'd become heavily in debt.

He looked over at Ethan. "You know all this?"

His friend nodded. "She told me all of it, at least as much as she knows. Just keep reading."

Anyway, whatever happened, they all think I have the pieces. Two men came to the house, but I found out ahead of time that they were coming. Deanne and I hid in the attic until they left, but then we hightailed it out of there. It's not safe for me to be anywhere in Michigan right now. I have to disappear until this is all over. Some pretty nasty men are looking for me, so I'm going to find a place to hide.

I had no idea where to go, but I knew I had to keep Deanne safe. As long as I am around her, that won't happen. I have to hide somewhere until Craig is caught and the items are recovered. If I'd stayed, I'm sure I would have been arrested and then what would happen? I don't have the money to hire a fancy lawyer, and I needed to protect Deanne.

So many emotions slammed into Dino. Shock. Anger. And yes, something else. Something he didn't want to identify.

You'll love our daughter, Dino. She's a wonderful little girl. The best. Please keep her safe.

Jen

Dino sat and stared at the letter for a long time. Shock, anger, uncertainty, and fear for Jen and Deanne swirled in him as if driven by an out-of-control motor. He looked at Ethan again. "I can't believe she didn't ever tell me about Deanne. If she was here in front of me…"

Ethan shook his head. "Don't even go there. When she learned she was pregnant, you were hardly on the list of good daddy candidates. You know that as well as I do. You were content with your life and would have resented having to change anything. At least, that was the act you put on."

"I hate to admit that you're right, but still…I mean, fuck it all, it's my kid."

"Who you probably would have resented the hell out of at the time. If you want Deanne to know the truth, you'd better be prepared for a long-term commitment that you can put a hundred percent into. Kids are very perceptive. You don't want her to wind up hating you."

He hated the fact that his friend was right.

"So you have no idea where Jen is?"

"None, and I am sorry as shit to have to say it. I never thought she'd run like that, much less memorize my security code to do it. And I know sorry doesn't cut it. I was sloppy and careless. Not my usual mode."

"You had no reason to suspect what she'd do," Lisa pointed out. "I didn't either. But the point is, she's in danger, and that means Deanne could be, too. That's why Jen left her here and why she told us you're her father. So we'd protect her."

"Wait a minute." Dino set his mug on the table. There was something niggling around in the back of his mind. Something he suddenly didn't want to acknowledge. "Maybe the girl isn't even mine. Maybe Jen just said that because…"

Lisa turned and held up a hand. "Wait until you see her. There's no doubt, I promise you."

Dino ground his teeth. If it really was true, Deanne could be a target for his own enemies as well as whatever Jen was mixed up in. He needed to make sure she was safe.

"Okay, everyone. Food's ready. Let's talk while we eat. Dino, you need to settle yourself down before we bring Deanne in."

"Aren't the kids eating with us?" He glared at her.

She shook her head. "All this testosterone might not be good for their digestion. Anyway, they already had breakfast. Sit. Eat. Listen while Ethan fills you in a little more."

As they shoveled in the food, Ethan repeated everything Jen had told him the night before, expanding on what she said in the letter.

"Did she tell you what kind of proof they have?" Dino demanded. "And how it all came out?"

"According to what she told me," Ethan answered, "the museum's art director was looking for the latest shipment for a showing he's putting together. He went to Craig and asked him where it was. Craig said they'd never received it. The art director has a hard-on for Craig, so he checked with the shipping company himself. Sure enough, they gave him a copy of the receipt for goods signed by Sutherland. So he went to Jen who went to Craig who blew her off. But the art director went to the chairman of the board, and that's when the shit hit the fan."

"Why would they think Jen had them hidden?" Dino asked.

"Because Craig Sutherland told everyone if something happened to the items, she was probably the one who had them. It was the only logical answer. That she must have intercepted the shipment before he could accept it. She overheard him telling someone on the phone, and the men searching her house said the same thing. Meanwhile, Sutherland's in the wind. But she's most concerned about Deanne, which is how she ended up here."

"What a piece of crap," Mike spit out.

"Amen to that."

"I'd like to find out more about the card game Sutherland mentioned," Ethan said. "Jen heard him say he thought it was a setup, and he could have been right. If the players are the uber wealthy elite, they'd only have one reason to invite someone like Sutherland to play. To get his balls in a wringer and squeeze him to smuggle in antiquities illegally."

"Not an unusual situation," Dino agreed. "Okay. We have two things going here. The first is to find Jen before someone else does. The second is to dig into this artifact smuggling thing and the card game. The FBI is already all over the smuggling, and we have to find Sutherland and the missing pieces before they do. That sounds like a big mess, and people who pay for that kind of stuff illegally are not nice about being crossed. If we don't get answers, Jen will never be safe."

"And how do you propose to do that?" Lisa wanted to know. "That's a project for more than one man."

"The first thing I need to do," Dino told them, "is get home, pull in my Blackwater crew, and get a plan together."

"Yes, you do." Ethan nodded. "You all did a great job rescuing Jamie, not to mention the contract work you do for both the CIA and Guardian. But to dig into what's going on and locate Jen, we're going to need more resources."

"We?" Dino raised an eyebrow. "Ethan, I can't ask you to jump into this. You have a family to consider now."

"Dino." Lisa leaned forward in her seat. "We're all family. You'd do the same for Ethan. He'd never sit by and not help with this."

"But—"

"No buts."

"You get the Blackwater crew together as soon as we're back in Key West," Ethan told him. "And I do mean we. I'm going with you." He held up a hand. "You have to find Jen before these assholes do, but someone needs to track down everyone else and find out who's doing what. That will be me with your guys. No argument. But I also think we should bring Guardian in on this, too. They have resources we don't, and they'd be really pissed if you didn't ask them for help."

A kaleidoscope of emotions flashed across Dino's face. "I think they have bigger and better things to occupy them."

"Bullshit," Ethan growled. "You're one of their best private contractors and a friend as well. So shut up and let me call them."

Dino hesitated a long moment before he nodded. "Okay. You're right. That would be a big help. They can dig out information better than you or me. And listen, I can pay whatever their going rate is."

"You can discuss that with Reno and Nick. But like you said, they have assets we're going to need, and you know you can trust these guys. Plus, I want them to put a full security team here at the farm while I'm gone. We can't take any chances by leaving this place unprotected. I'd bring in an army if I thought it would make a difference."

"Good. They're dependable and don't fuck things up."

"Language," Lisa reminded him.

"No one heard me except you guys," Dino grumbled.

But, at that exact moment, they heard the sound of feet running in the hallway and two little people skidded into the kitchen. Dino recognized Jamie Caine at once. He was Lisa's son from her first marriage to a man who had turned out to be a drug dealer and had kidnapped Jamie. Ethan, with Dino's Blackwater crew, had rescued him, the drug dealer was killed, and when Ethan and Lisa married, he adopted Jamie. The few times Dino had seen them, they seemed like a very happy family.

And each time he was struck with a feeling of

jealousy.

But it was the young girl who really made his heart stop. Long golden-brown hair hung down in a neat ponytail and framed a heart-shaped face with chocolate brown eyes. He could have sworn he was looking at Jen as a very young girl. Even the shape of the face was the same. But the color of the eyes and the high cheekbones were his. He was mesmerized, rooted to his chair. Poleaxed.

Holy shit!

"Dino?" Lisa's voice finally pierced his stupor.

"Uh, yeah."

"I'd like you to meet Deanne LaCroix. Jennifer's daughter. You know. Our friend, Jennifer."

So that answered his question about how much the little girl knew. Almost nothing.

"Hello." The word came out as barely a whisper.

Dino hated the fear that shadowed her eyes. What the hell had been going on?

He finally found his voice. "Nice to meet you, Deanne. I'm Dino Brancuzzi, a friend of—"

"Ethan's and mine," Lisa interrupted, flashing a look at Dino.

Deanne studied him with an intense, questioning look. "Do you know my mom?"

"Yes, I do." He flashed a glance at Lisa that said, Well, I'm not gonna lie. "I think very highly of her."

She still hadn't moved from her spot next to Jamie.

"I think she's in trouble. We had to leave our home and drive all the way here. Some not nice men were in our house, and we had to hide from them. It took us a long time to get here."

Dino, who actually didn't spend a lot of time

around kids, wanted nothing more than to wrap her in his arms and tell her everything would be fine. "If she is, we're going to help get her out of it. That's a promise."

"Th-that would be really wonderful."

She looked at Jamie and reached for his hand. There was no mistaking the fear in her eyes. Dino had to restrain himself from telling her who he really was. Damn Jen anyway for keeping this a secret. Although, up until today, he wouldn't have told him either.

Deanne didn't answer, just looked at Dino, fear in her eyes. "Do you know where my mom is? She said she had to leave to do an errand, but you'd look out for me."

Dino was torn between wanting to curse Jen soundly and thank her for taking the danger away from their daughter. Daughter! He was still getting used to the word.

Lisa pulled Deanne into a gentle hug. "And we're definitely going to do that. Mr. Brancuzzi and Ethan are going to make sure she's safe and you, too. Now, how about a snack for you guys."

Deanne didn't look as if she was too convinced, but she nodded.

Dino watched Lisa hand them juice boxes and some kind of treat. Then Jamie, who seemed to be Deanne's protector, nudged her toward the game room. The sight of it gave him a weird lump in his throat.

"She has my eyes." Dino stared after the two kids.

"And your chin," Ethan pointed out. "So she's probably just as stubborn as you are."

Dino raked his fingers through his hair. "We have to find Jen so we can protect her and get those two together."

"And we will," Ethan assured him.

"You've never failed at anything yet, Dino." It was the first thing Mike had said since the conversation began. "You won't now."

"Amen to that," Ethan agreed. "Well. Good thing it's Saturday, and there aren't any classes today. And I'm going to cancel the ones for next week. I'd just as soon not have anybody on the grounds until this is resolved and Jen is safe and sound."

Lisa walked back into the kitchen. "Okay, they're all set for a while. I'll leave you all to get to it."

"How much do you know about the antiquities market?" Dino asked when they each had full mugs of coffee again.

"I had some…situations dealing with it a few years ago," Ethan told him. "And I know Guardian has been involved in a couple of cases with it. Another reason to bring them in. I understand, though, it's escalated recently. I do know that items stolen from museums and archeological digs and smuggled into the country are worth more than diamonds. Collectors will pay any price for them. And where they were stolen from dictates how high the price goes. If Sutherland needed a hunk of money, that's the place to get it."

Dino frowned. "Jen and Deanne are in a great deal of danger. If her boss is running from a gambling ring as well as a stolen antiquities situation the stakes have accelerated. Not to mention the FBI being involved. Sutherland could hang a frame on Jen, and she could end up getting arrested even though she's innocent. Mike, call the crew and give them a heads up to meet us at the boat."

"If we don't take care of this," Ethan agreed, "Jen and Deanne will never have another day of peace in their lives."

Okay. Fate was giving him another chance. He'd better not fuck it up.

Dino drained the last of his coffee. "Then let's get busy."

Chapter Five

The day was mentally exhausting for Dino. He was still trying to get his head around the mess that was Jen's situation and the fact that he had a daughter. Obviously, when she left him, she'd gone as far as she could. Michigan was about as far from Key West as possible without leaving the States. And she'd been lucky enough to get a job that utilized her skills and work history. But had she lacked trust in him so much that she ran far and fast without a word?

Yes, you asshole. She wasn't going to put herself and her daughter—your daughter—in danger, because you liked playing spy games.

He had a lot to make up for when he found her, not the least of which was admitting to both of them the feelings he'd had for her all these years. He just hoped to fuck she listened to him.

While they finished breakfast, Ethan called Guardian Security and gave them a brief rundown. Certainly, there was no agency better equipped to help them and he and Dino both had a history with them, Ethan as an agent and Dino doing contract work for them. Guardian had the resources to dig out information and supply additional manpower if needed.

Additionally, he and Ethan would both be gone before the end of the day, and leaving the Caine compound unprotected wasn't even a question. There was no one else they could trust security to. So half an hour after Ethan made his call, the two senior partners who had created Guardian, Reno Sullivan and Nick Vanetta, arrived at the house. Everyone gathered around the big kitchen table while Ethan and Dino filled in the details for them.

Reno nodded. "We discussed this on the way out here, and based on the situation, we're going to have rotating crews of four, changing every eight hours so they'll always be fresh. Three outside, one inside. The senior team leader will be here at all times. Ethan, you can put him up in your barracks back there?"

"We've got a guest room in the house he can use," Ethan said. "His sleep will be sporadic, so he needs to be comfortable."

"Thanks for that," Nick said. "We want security here to be tight."

"Whatever it takes." Dino gave the tall, dark-haired man a piercing look. "The cost is no object. I can handle whatever it is. Since neither Ethan nor I will be here, we need your very best."

"You'll have it," Nick assured him. "But you know all our operatives are top tier. We don't settle for any less." He grinned. "I'd say that's why we hire you now and then, but I'd hate for you to get a big head."

Dino grinned. "As long as everyone else is as good as me." The smile disappeared. "You know where I'm coming from."

"We do." Reno nodded. "And it's all good."

"And again," Dino repeated, "price is no object."

"There won't be a charge for this," Reno told him. "And for god's sake, please don't try to argue. We never charge for family business, and you're both part of the Guardian Security family. Now. Let's talk about what else you need."

Nick called the head of Guardian's tech unit and sent him a list to get started on some heavy digging. He was grinning when he hung up.

"Jack Smiley says whatever you need, it's yours," Nick told Dino. "He'll get started right away."

Dino just nodded. He'd worked with Jack Smiley a long time ago. He remembered a time in Thailand on a very, very, very black mission, before Guardian and Blackwater. Smiley had stepped away from his computer for that one and about got his ass shot off, and Ethan dragged him out of the line of fire, even though he'd been shot himself. He'd brought him with him when he joined Guardian, and when he left, Smiley stayed on. It seemed he'd made a real niche for himself.

"You brought him to Guardian," Nick reminded him, "and now he's the head of our computer department. He typed Craig Sutherland's name in the search box while we were on the phone. According to him, this thing has been all over the media in Michigan the last couple of days. It seems his disappearance is big news, him being the director of a very high-profile museum and all."

Dino snorted. "I'll bet. How did it all explode?"

"They've tried to keep an eye on Sutherland," Reno added, "but he gave even the Feds the slip. They checked his house, and there's no trace of him."

An itchy feeling crawled up Dino's neck. "Did they find anything?" But even as he asked the question, he knew the answer.

Nick shook his head. "Smiley said, from what the cops reported, it looked like a bunch of vandals had gone through it. The place was all torn up. Furniture smashed. And no sign of what happened to the wife and kid. He'll get into the cloud and download Sutherland's phone and computer, too. But meanwhile he scoured every place for anything on what's happening. It's big news, at least up in Michigan and in the art world."

"What about Jen?" Dino asked. "Any word about her status?"

"Yeah, damn it. She's listed as a missing person of interest."

"No fucking way." Dino slammed his hand on the table.

Nick held up a hand. "We all know that, but this makes it even more imperative to get at the truth, which is another good reason you called us. At least, they didn't come right out and accuse her to the public. Right now, the speculation is Sutherland left his wife and ran off with Jen. We should leave that out there so nobody gets in the way of our investigation. And luckily, for some reason, there's no mention of Deanne."

"Better for her that there isn't." Dino gritted his teeth. "But it means the whole world is looking for Jen. They might as well have focused a spotlight on her. No wonder she disappeared. I have to find her before anyone else does." He pushed back from the table." Okay, while you guys are doing your thing, I'm going to make another call."

But he walked out to the back porch to make this one. Better that no one should hear. Guardian could dig pretty deep into the antiquities world, but Dino had another contact that could dig with a bigger shovel. In the world of dark activities, he'd acquired some very key contacts along the way. Time to tap into one of them now. And then maybe some others. The call was to a number he hadn't reached out to in so many years he wasn't even sure it still worked, but it was his only place to start. The voice that answered was hard and uninflected.

"You must have the wrong number."

"If you're reading from the caller ID, you'd think so," Dino replied. "I want to speak to Martin Van Dine."

"You must have the wrong number," the voice repeated. "There's no such person here."

"Well, if you should happen to stumble over him, please tell him Dino Brancuzzi would like to hear from him at this number."

"I wouldn't sit around and wait for it," the voice said before it clicked off.

Dino shoved a hand through his hair and let out a sigh. He only had a ten percent chance Van Dine would return the call. He didn't even know if the man was still alive.

Years ago, he'd had to make a choice on a mission. His orders were to take out two men running a lot of money to insurgent groups in African countries. Trapped in a difficult circumstance, he'd had to let one go in order to take out the other. He'd chosen to let Van Dine make his escape. The way he looked at it, the man owed him. And if anyone could dig into the black side of the antiquities market, Van Dine would be the one.

"Will you guys still be around for lunch," Lisa asked Nick and Reno.

"If it's your famous stew, my mouth is already watering," Reno told her, "but sadly we're heading back to the office. We want to see what Smiley has dug up and also send the first security team out here."

"But we'll take a raincheck," Nick added. "Count on it. Look for the crew early this afternoon."

"Will do. And thanks again."

Dino watched the car pull away, then turned to Ethan and Mike. "We need to head for Key West as soon as the security team gets here and we show them around. I want to get my crew together and start figuring out where Jen might be hiding. We were together long enough that I got a sense of where she'd like to go if she could and why."

"And that is?"

"The Caribbean and its multitude of islands. She's familiar with the environment, and she has contacts. Although, I don't know how many are active after ten years. Unless she's had a change of heart in ten years, it gives us a place to start."

"And what if she decided she'd rather go to Alaska."

Dino managed his first real smile of the day. "Not likely. She hates cold weather. And I'm sure ten years in Michigan made the Caribbean seem a lot more appealing."

Lunch was not a leisurely meal. Dino was torn between getting his ass in gear and dragging everything out as long as he could so he could be with Deanne. Every second he got to spend with her was a gift. Amazing that a man who never thought there was a place in his life for children was suddenly unwilling to leave this one for even a few seconds, let alone days. Someone had once told him that when the child was your own flesh and blood, all other thoughts went out the window. How true that was.

They had just finished when a buzzer sounded in the hallway, announcing someone at the gate at the end of the driveway.

"I'll get it." Ethan pushed back from the table. "I gave Nick a code word for them."

"I'll go with you." Dino rose, also, and followed Ethan out to the hallway.

"Yes?" Ethan pushed the button for the gate intercom.

"We're here from Guardian," a male voice said. "The code word is Quintana."

Ethan nodded and pushed the button to unlock the gate. Dino followed him out to the porch, watching as a black SUV came up the driveway and parked in the area next to the house.

When did black SUVs become the identifying vehicles for security agents?

Four men climbed out, all wearing jeans and soft collared shirts with the Guardian Security logo on them. The lead man shook hands with Ethan. Dino didn't miss the air of camaraderie or the utter respect these men had for his friend. Someday, he'd drag it out of him what he did for Guardian. But not today.

"Good to see you again, my man. Sorry it has to be under these circumstances."

Ethan nodded. "No kidding. But thanks for doing this."

"Hey. Guardian owes you a big debt. This is barely a down payment."

"Meet Dino Brancuzzi," Ethan told him. "He was part of Guardian for a while before you joined the agency. Dino, this is Dan Mora, one of the senior security team leaders at Guardian."

Dan introduced the rest of his men, and everyone shook hands.

"I'd like to walk the area outside before we check the inside of the house," Dan told Ethan. "I know you have the premier security setup here, but you and I both know there's always a chance for penetration. I want my men familiar with every possible access to the property, just in case."

Ethan nodded. "I agree. Dino, you might want to walk with us and familiarize yourself with it, so you'll have a visual. I know Deanne's safety will be topmost on your mind."

"Thanks. I'll feel a lot better seeing everything for myself."

As they headed toward the rear of the house, Nick stopped short when he spotted the chopper.

"Ethan, you buy a new toy to play with?"

Ethan shook his head. "No, that belongs to a friend of Dino's who flew him up here from Key West. Okay let's get moving."

An hour later, the security check was complete, and the men had carried their gear into the bunkhouse Ethan had built behind the main house as part of the training complex. Ethan packed a Go-Bag, and while he said a quiet goodbye to Lisa, going over everything with her, Dino took advantage of every minute with Deanne. His heart ached for all the years he missed and the life he'd chosen for himself that kept Jen from telling him about her.

"Do me a favor, will you?" He spoke to Lisa in a low voice. "Can you get some shots of Deanne with your phone and send them to me? Please?"

Understanding flashed in her eyes. "Of course. Now get going and find Jen and fix her problem."

If only it was that simple.

Then Dino and Mike piled into the helocopter, and in minutes they were in the air headed toward Key West. It seemed they'd just lifted off before they were getting ready to land. Mike parked the plane at Key West Tours at the airport.

"You calling a meeting?" he asked.

Dino nodded. "In about thirty minutes. We're not wasting time."

"I'll contact the crew and meet you on the boat. That work?"

Dino nodded. "Yes. And thanks."

Dino retrieved his car from the parking area where he'd left it. As usual, the streets were clogged with tourist traffic, but he'd been navigating it for so long, it didn't bother him. Finally, they pulled into the driveway next to his cottage. Ethan had been here a couple of times so the Key West cottage was familiar to him. Painted a dazzling white, with shutters and doors a soft blue, it butted right up to the sidewalk with only three steps leading to a wide porch. Two rockers sat invitingly to one side of the front door.

Dino hoped this all ended in a good place for everyone, and he could sit on this porch with Jen and Deanne, looking toward a future he'd never dreamed he could have. But the first order of business was to find Jen, and he was itching to get started. He led the way up the steps to the porch, unlocked the front door, and waved Ethan inside. "You know where the guest room is, so dump your stuff there, and we'll get to work."

While Ethan carried his bag into the room, Dino

looked around, trying to see the place through Jen's eyes if—no, not if but when—he found her and brought her here. The bungalow was small, but he kept it scrupulously clean. The walls were a cool cream color, and the floors were terra cotta tiles. The kitchen was small but efficient and led onto a back porch shaded by two very tall trees.

He could visualize the three of them there. And damn it! He was going to make that happen.

At that moment, his cell phone dinged with a text from Mike.

"All present, accounted for, and on their way to the boat."

Good. He felt better already knowing his core team was on board. Angel Rodriguez, Ben Ramsey, and Octavio March had worked with Dino in other lifetimes. When he'd put the Blackwater crew together in the beginning, they were the first he tapped. No matter the situation, they'd handle it.

He always held these meetings on the boat, on the water, where there was no danger of eavesdroppers. He and Ethan piled into his car again, and fifteen minutes later, they were pulling into the gravel parking lot of the marina Dino owned. Being the owner was better than renting, because it gave him control over the situation, a good thing when Blackwater went dark. He checked the small building that served as the office for Blackwater Charters, making sure everything was still secure, before heading down to the end of the dock.

A couple of people waved and called to him. He waved back, but he and Ethan just kept walking. His team was already waiting for him, relaxing on deck as if getting ready for a sunset fishing trip. The ladder had already been dropped over the side to the dock, so he and Ethan climbed aboard.

"Ready for a little trip?" he asked the others, maintaining the image of a casual sunset trip.

They all nodded and exchanged greetings.

"Go on and get a cold drink while I move us out of here."

He unlocked the cabin so the men could get their drinks while he climbed up into the wheelhouse, Ethan following him. Just as he was about to turn the key, his phone dinged, and he saw Lisa's name. He opened the message, and there were the pictures of Deanne he'd asked for. Five of them. God, she was so sweet and adorable. His daughter! He made a silent vow—him, the avowed bachelor—that when this was over and everyone was safe, he was going to build a life with Jen and Deanne, if Jen would let him. He was prepared to do whatever it took to convince her.

That's right, the old horn dog wanted to settle down. Big shock.

So many emotions were battling inside him that he didn't realize the boat still wasn't moving until Ethan nudged him. "You can stare at those when we're back at the house. Right now, if you want to help her, we need to get down to business."

"Right, right, right."

Dino yelled for Octavio and Angel to cast off the lines for him, and he hit the ignition switch. The very expensive powerful twin motors turned over smoothly, and he eased away from the dock and past the entrance to the marina.

He could think of nothing but finding Jen. The important thing was to keep her safe and out of harm's way. That asshole Sutherland had set her up as a target and that was unacceptable. When he got his hands on the snake—and he would, sooner or later—he'd teach him a lesson he'd never forget.

Everyone was below deck, waiting for him while they headed out to open water. This was always the best place to meet to discuss things he didn't want overheard. His house was not set up with the electronics they needed to do their research, plus he never liked to advertise that something might be going on in there. He never knew who might be trying to keep an eye on him.

Dino was obsessed with secrecy, something necessary in the dark contracts he took, so he always looked for some isolated spot to drop anchor for a while. And now, totally focused on finding Jen, he needed to stay under the radar as much as possible. Ethan and the Blackwater crew would concentrate on finding Sutherland and tracing who his new antiquities buyer was. Ethan would handle all that with the Blackwater Crew.

No one spoke as they moved smoothly out into the Gulf. When they were half an hour from the marina Dino steered the boat into an isolated cove, then dropped anchor, turned off the engines, and joined everyone down in the cabin.

When Dino had bought the boat, he'd gone for the best he could get, so the lounge area they all sat in came outfitted with, among other things, a large screen television set into one wall. It was also outfitted with its own satellite system.

"Okay, everyone. Let's get busy. I have a feeling we're already behind the game."

"I've got a map of the Caribbean up on the screen."

Angel, who was sitting on the couch, pointed to the wall across from him. He clicked some keys on his open laptop on the small table in front of the couch. "I don't think she'd go where there's a lot of publicized activity," he added. "Places where high profile people take their vacations."

"She wouldn't think to lose herself in a crowd?" Octavio asked. "I know you said she likes the Caribbean and is very familiar with it. That's why we're focusing there. But wouldn't she go to some place she had a history with, like St. Thomas?"

Dino shook his head. "Angel's right. Jen's smart. She knows anyone looking for her would figure she'd try to lose herself in the places with the largest populations and the most activities. Change the way she looks a little. Lose herself in the crowd. Also the people looking for her could put out feelers to their friends who hang out there. No, that atmosphere is one she'd stay away from. However, I'm sure she has a lot of contacts from her years on St. Thomas, and she might have tried to reach out to one of them for suggestions."

And wouldn't it just fucking help if he'd paid better attention so he remembered who some of them were now. He pulled out his laptop from the messenger bag he'd brought, booted it up, and pulled up a search engine.

"Some background first," he said as he was typing. "Ten years ago, when I was taking every wildass, dangerous assignment I could find, I met a woman who is every man's wet dream. But in those days, danger was still my drug of choice. I was too much of an adrenaline junkie to deal with a wife. I thought I had plenty of time to get it out of my system and settle down."

"Didn't we all," Ethan snorted.

"Only Jennifer LaCroix got tired of waiting for me to grow up. One day she was there, the next she was gone."

"Just up and left?" Octavio asked.

"You got it. But it was no more than I deserved. It turns out, though, she had a very good reason."

"And that was?" Angel prompted.

"She'd discovered she was pregnant."

Mike already knew the answer, but the other three stared at him.

"You have a kid?" Octavio asked at last.

"How did you find out?" Angel wanted to know.

In short, concise sentences Dino brought them up to date about Jen's situation, her trip to Ethan and Lisa's, her disappearance and leaving Deanne behind.

"We've got a multiple prong operation going here," he told them as he tapped away on the keyboard. "One. Locating Jen. Two, finding Sutherland and the artifacts. Three, finding out who's behind all of this, both his regular "client" and the new one. For all we know, he could have met his latest money man, handed over the goods, the guy killed him and made the body disappear. If that's what happened, we're left with nothing. So that means number four, finding where those missing pieces are now. Did he actually turn them over to his new "client," which makes identifying that person critical?"

Angel snorted. "That all? Want us to find a permanent cure for COVID-19 while we're at it?"

"If you could." Dino gave him a hard glare. "But I'll settle for discovering who's behind this shitstorm."

"Okay." Octavio stretched. "Where do you wanna start? Where would Jen go?"

"Big question," Dino growled. The clicking of the keys sounded unusually loud in the quiet area. Then, suddenly, the screen lit up with a document, then more documents. He went through them one at a time. "Okay, I've brought up basic information here." He studied the documents. "He's been the director of the Alcarez Museum in the Detroit area for ten years. They specialize in South American and Caribbean artifacts. He's responsible for handling all the shipments as they come in and is in the best position to get his hands on things."

"So what's the hinky part?" Octavio asked. "Is he using the shipments to disguise bringing illegal drugs into the country for a cartel or what? What's he selling to his so-called customers?"

"Something totally different," Ethan told them. "Like using the incoming shipments of artifacts to include smuggled items he then sells for big bucks. Jen says he's the one who made the shipment disappear. The museum's in an uproar and the board is on the warpath."

Dino nodded. "No shit. But Sutherland pointed the finger in Jen's direction to take the heat off him and was getting ready to get the fuck out of there."

"Leaving her to take the blame," Ethan added.

"Not to mention," Dino went on, "his regular customer is big time pissed off. According to Jen, Sutherland's using the money to play in a high stakes private poker game twice a month. We need to find out how he got into that poker game. My educated guess is he's a bad player and whoever runs the game knew it and targeted him so they could get his balls in a wringer. Run up his losings and force him to smuggle antiquities for them. Lots of rich people like forbidden goods. They don't care if no one but them ever sees them."

"And the money they pay him covers his gambling losses and gives him a new stake," Octavio guessed.

"That's what I think."

And they all looked at each other.

Chapter Six

Angel leaned forward. "So Sutherland's got his dick in a twist."

"He needed to get the hell out of there. He chose the wrong people to double cross this time and he needed a fall guy." Dino clicked more keys. "And you can bet whoever his regular customer was is pissed as hell and after him like a heat seeking missile."

"That's what Jen told me," Ethan added.

"And now she's on the run," Dino growled. "I'm heading out to look for her in the Caribbean. When Jen and I were...together...she loved the Caribbean. I know she's found a hiding place on one of them, and I'm going to dig it out."

"Guardian's going to check out all the players for us," Ethan told them, "and keep feeding us the info." He clicked more keys, and a newspaper article appeared on the screen. "Here's the picture of Sutherland, and there's also one of Welborn."

"Typical businessman who looks legit but maybe isn't," Angel commented. "Any gossip about him at all?"

"Thus the field trip," Ethan said.

"You two"—Dino pointed back and forth between Angel and Octavio—"are going to find out where Sutherland and those artifacts are and get your hands on them, whatever you have to do." He looked at the third member of his team. "Ben, you're command central while we're gone."

Ben nodded. "Got it."

Ben managed the electronics setup with an expert touch and ran the marina like a well-oiled machine. They all knew that without the right person running those comms they'd could be dead in the water.

Dino looked at the map again. "There's at least twenty islands there that she could land on, especially if she managed to connect with an old contact from St. Thomas. We have to start searching someplace, so let's start with the islands that are the most off the radar and see what we can find out about them."

He glanced over at Ethan. "You got anything?"

"Just got an email from Nick Vanetta," he answered. "Smiley's pulled together some stuff on Roger Welborn. Jen's guess is he's Sutherland's primary customer on illegal goods."

Dino lifted an eyebrow. "Does he have any info on who Sutherland's new customer might be? If there even is one?"

Ethan shook his head. "No, but they're still digging. You and I both know that no one is completely invisible."

"Yeah, no kidding."

"Okay." Angel looked at the others. "Time to get moving. Right, Dino? Twist some wrists to get the names of people involved. Rich doesn't make you honest."

Dino barked a laugh, "No, shit, Dick Tracy."

"I'll make plans for the Michigan trip," Ethan told the others.

"I'll call Mike Hogan," Octavio said, "and tell him

what I need. He'll pick a good place to drop us off, and we'll take it from there. Dino, okay if we keep him on standby?"

"Absolutely," Dino said. "Let's get moving."

Within minutes, they were on their way. It had turned dark while they were sitting below in the cabin, so he turned on the running lights.

He heard someone come up behind him and, without turning, knew it was Ethan.

"You sure you don't want anyone with you on this?" his friend asked.

"Positive." He could move faster, hide better, and get what he needed more quickly if he was solo.

"Are you okay?" Ethan asked the question in a quiet voice.

Dino shrugged. "As much as I can be, discovering the woman I…had a relationship with is being hunted by killers and I have a daughter I didn't even know existed."

A relationship with. That was certainly a sanitized way of putting it. Whenever he'd thought of Jennifer LaCroix over the years, heat surged through him and his dick begged for relief.

From the time they met, he had spent every spare minute with her. And every time he was between assignments, he flew down to see her and they fucked each other's brains out. Besides being fun to be with and smart, Jen was a caring person, always concerned about other people. She had a special way about her that drew people to her like a magnet.

And then, without warning, she was gone. Just gone. Quit her job and disappeared into the stratosphere. He'd been irritated and disappointed and pulled out the stops looking for her. Finally, pissed off at himself for getting so caught up in this, he'd just shut his mind down as best he could and tried to forget about her.

And how has that worked out?

He needed to follow up on his calls. He pulled his phone from his pocket, but before making calls, he pulled up the pictures of Deanne, memorizing every feature, every expression. He saw so much of Jen in her, the slight figure, the thick blonde hair, the saucy dimples. But he also saw himself in her, in the dark brown eyes, the arched eyebrows, and the defiant set of the chin.

He'd missed nine years of her life because he'd made Jen feel so uncertain about a relationship with him that she hadn't felt she could share with him. Not a good commentary on the person he'd been then.

But what about the person he was now?

When he found Jen he was going to apologize for everything he hadn't done. And then he was going to lay himself bare to convince her that they could be a family. Because, cards on the table, he was in love with Jennifer LaCroix. And now with their beautiful daughter.

Well, then. He'd better get his ass in gear.

****

Time to just suck it up and find a place to hide.

Jen talked to herself as she maneuvered through traffic. She had to make a decision about where to go and make it fast. Her first inclination was to return to St. Thomas in the Virgin Islands, but she wasn't sure if anyone she knew was still there. She'd made it a point to break off contact with everyone when she fled to

Michigan. Of course, it might be better for her if they weren't there. Some of the people she'd hung around were less than trustworthy, and right now, she had to be extra careful.

But she needed someplace to go. Someplace in the Caribbean where she knew how to hide at least until the worst of this was over. It was where she felt the most comfortable. And also where she knew how to adapt and make herself invisible.

At least, Deanne would be safe. Ethan would make sure of that. She could have tried looking for Dino, but there just hadn't been enough time. Besides, Ethan was a safer bet, because she had no idea what Dino's feelings for her were after all these years. She just prayed that he'd open his heart to their daughter when he met her and love her and keep her safe.

The first thing Jen had done after leaving Ethan's was stop at a big box store, the kind that was open twenty-four/seven and buy two cell phones. Burner phones that would not connect back to her. Then she looked for a place to hole up and analyze her situation. She found one that was plain, clean, cheap, and convenient to a lot of things she needed. And lucky for her, right across the street was a convenience store open twenty-four/seven. She loaded up with muffins and brownies and two large coffees. It was too early to call people and she'd need the caffeine and sugar to keep going.

Back in her motel room, she opened one of the coffees, blew on it, and took a sip, letting the hot liquid slide down her throat. She bit into one of the muffins she'd bought then studied the tiny list she'd had tucked in her wallet. Time to figure out who would be most willing to help her. She hoped she didn't have to go through the whole list.

She waited impatiently until eight o'clock before starting her calls. The first one, to her mind, was the most logical. She and Lexie Green had been friends, and of all the people Jen had walked away from, except for Dino, Lexie was the one she regretted the most. She wasn't even sure if the woman would speak to her after all this time.

The number still worked, but all she got was a voice mail message. "Hi, it's Lexie. Can't answer right now. You know what to do."

She was sure the "what to do" meant leaving a voice mail message, but she didn't want to do that. She'd go down the rest of the list, then try again.

But the rest of the names on her list all turned out to be dead ends. She'd been right about St. Thomas. The people she knew were all gone. Phones disconnected. All except for Lexie, who hadn't answered but at least still had the same number. They had been friends, although not close ones, but close enough that Jen could reach out after all these years. Besides, she'd gotten the woman out of a sticky situation a time or two, because that's who she was. Maybe Lexie would still remember them.

And Jen needed a place to go and a way to get there that would allow her to conceal her gun. She couldn't afford to be without it, not with the people after her.

She lay back on the bed and closed her eyes, fighting fatigue and hoping Lexie would call back very soon. She needed to get someplace where no one would look for her and fast.

Unbidden, an image of Dino floated across her brain. Tall, lean, and muscular, with hair below his collar and a scruff beard, he looked every bit the adventurer that he was. And sexy. Let's not forget sexy. The very first time she'd laid eyes on him at the special event, her nipples had hardened and the walls of her sex had spasmed with unexpected need.

She knew at once he was trouble. Her intuition told her to grab her purse and get the hell out of there, but her hunger for him buried that intuition. At least she hadn't taken him home with her after knowing him for only five minutes. Probably the only smart thing she did. But then, when she had…

The sight of him naked was even more than she had dreamed. Flat abs, broad shoulders, narrow hips, and a cock that she wasn't sure she could even get her fingers around. She wanted to smooth her palm over his beard and run her fingers through the thickness of his hair.

But it wasn't just his physical appeal that grabbed her. No, damn it. From the moment she laid eyes on Dino Brancuzzi, her emotions had been swirling around and her heart was in danger of being lost to him. And she couldn't seem to make herself do anything about it.

"Those must be some heavy thoughts," he teased, running his knuckle along the line of her jaw.

Then he licked the seam of her lips, pushing until she opened for him, and he slid his tongue inside. Her entire body responded, like a flower opening to the sun. This wasn't just sex, no matter how much she tried to tell herself it was. Dino Brancuzzi invaded every inch of her, every emotion. She had to be very careful, because she'd known from the start he wasn't a permanent type of man. He was an adventurer, who skated the edge of danger and wasn't looking for anything beyond a way to take the edge off.

Be careful, she kept telling herself. You lose your heart to him and he'll run away with it.

But deep inside, she knew it was too late. She'd lost it the first night he came home with her. She'd have to do her best to deal with the fallout when it finally came to the end, but she wasn't ready to think of it yet. Right now, she just wanted to enjoy every minute of it.

She twined her tongue with his, relishing the taste of him and arching her naked body against his. The soft hair on his chest tickled her breasts, and his thick, hard cock pressed against her mound until she was sure it would leave an impression.

Inside me, she wanted to urge. Go inside me now.

They'd already shared two intense orgasms, and she was shocked to feel her body rousing itself for another one. Dino slid his hand down her side to her thigh and between her legs to rest on her mound. One finger eased between the lips and found her clit, where he…

Jen's eyes popped open, and her heart raced.

Shit!

What the hell was she doing, lying back on the bed with her hand inside her panties and rubbing her clit? Having hot dreams about Dino Brancuzzi, the man who'd run away with her heart. No, she was the one who'd run away, out of a need for self-protection. And now she was doing it again.

It had taken her a while and lots of discipline, but she'd finally managed to block him almost totally. Along with her feelings for him that she'd never allowed herself to indulge in. He wasn't a man for relationships. She'd gotten that message loud and clear. But the current situation brought everything back, and now her body ached and tingled as if the man himself had been here in bed with her.

Had she made a mistake in not telling him about Deanne?

No. She mentally shook her head.

She'd thought about it for a long time, weighing all the pros and cons, but not even all those months together had convinced her to tell him. Dino had had a permanent case of wandering feet. People who knew him had been surprised that their relationship had lasted as long as it had. His life was one long adventure, with no time for anything permanent, certainly not a child.

Creating a story for Deanne had been the most difficult. She didn't want to make Dino so unlikeable that if the time came when they connected—like now!—her daughter would not have a built-in hate for the man. She finally came up with the story that he did secret work for the government—not so far off—and was gone for very long periods of time. Also, because of the work he did, if people knew about her, they might try to hurt them so she had to keep them both safe.

She was still surprised that Deanne had bought it, even as she grew older. Then it occurred to her that maybe her daughter thought the truth was so bad she'd just accept the story. Jen's heart ached for the situation she'd created. What would happen now that Dino knew of Deanne's existence? How would he react?

Enough, already. She needed to get him out of her head and focus on her mission. Deanne was safe, and

Jen was sure Ethan and Lisa would tell Dino the whole story. It would probably be safer for all of them—and for her heart—if she found a place to go and stayed gone.

Picking up her phone, she tried Lexie's number again, and this time her friend answered.

"God, a voice from the past." Her surprise was obvious. "I thought maybe you were dead or something."

Or something.

But how lucky was it that the one person she could connect with was not unstable, not a prima donna, just a good solid person who wanted to enjoy life. She'd always been someone people could count on.

"You sure disappeared off the radar for a long time. Everything okay?"

Jen nibbled on her lip, wondering just how much she could tell her friend. She had been closer to Lexie than anyone else during her time on St. Thomas, but could she trust her?

"Yeah," she said at last. "I had some, uh, family issues that took a long time to handle."

"No shit." Lexie chuckled. "Ten years long. That must have been some family trouble if it took all this time to settle."

You have no idea.

"Some things just can't be hurried," she said. What a lame excuse.

"Well, I hope you got it done the way you wanted. By the way, what happened to that really sexy guy you hung out with now and then? Did you walk away from him, too?"

Yes, but I took part of him with me. "Didn't have

room for that, what with the family problems."

"So what's up that you call out of the blue? You looking to come back down this way?"

Jen drew in a breath and let it out slowly, reminding herself not to sound desperate. "Well, I decided I need to get my Caribbean mojo back, and I wanted to see what's going on. You still on St. Thomas? Everyone else seems to have left."

"Me, too, as a matter of fact, but only a couple of years ago. Decided I wanted something with a little less hustle."

"Oh?" If Lexie had left, she might be out of options, unless… "So where are you now?"

"Someplace a lot quieter and a lot less stressful but still a lot of fun. There's a small resort on a little island called Hermosa. Hermosa means beautiful in Spanish, and the first settlers thought it was so beautiful that's what they named it. It's right near the Cayman Islands but a lot less high-profile. Ever heard of it?"

"Hold on a second. Let me look it up."

Yes, there it was, tucked into the area of Turks and Caicos, a tiny little spit of land that probably got very little attention. Exactly what she needed.

"Holy crap, Lexie. How does anyone even know about it?" This would be perfect if she could work it out.

Lexie laughed. "Good question. They cater to families and small groups. Some of the people who came to St. Thomas during the last few years I was there talked about it, about wanting the flavor of the Caribbean with a lot less hustle. The visitors who come here like to avoid the high-profile places so they can just relax and have a good time."

"I'd think it was too quiet for you."

"Actually, I love it. Don't have a lot of the stress I had in my life on St. Thomas."

Jen frowned. "And you're working there? Doing what?"

"I manage the gift shop in the hotel. It's fun, and the people are very nice." There was a short pause. "If you're looking to come back down this way, I can tell you they don't have any museums down here or any places like it that you might want to work in."

"I've been out of the museum business for a while." Five days. "I actually like something with a lot less pressure."

"If you mean that, I happen to know the dive shop at the marina is losing their manager. That is a totally no stress gig."

"A dive shop?" Jen frowned. She and Dino had done some diving, but she was only mildly good at it. And she sure wasn't about to get a job at a museum where Roger Welborn could easily find her. "I know very little about diving."

"Oh, no teaching or anything," Lexie assured her. "They have instructors for that. They just need someone to keep the schedule, rent equipment, and sell odds and ends. Someone honest enough to handle the money. And I can vouch for you."

Well, it wasn't as if she could walk into any place on the mainland and ask for a job. She had no idea how far Roger Welborn's reach extended, but she'd bet, with his money, it went pretty far. And there was a good bet he'd never heard of a place as obscure as Hermosa. And hopefully, Dino hadn't either.

"Jen? You still there?"

"Yes. Yes, I am."

"Well? What do you think? It's a low-key place. Low pay but low expenses and maybe a good place to hang out while you recover from your, uh, family troubles."

Jen thought for another minute.

"How would I get there? I still have my passport, but…" Her words trailed off.

"But you don't want to bring your family troubles with you," Lexie guessed, a touch of irony in her voice. "Tell me the truth here, Jen. I need you to be honest with me. Will you be putting me or my friends here in a bad position?"

Jen couldn't deny it with a certainty, but it seemed highly unlikely.

"No. No, I won't."

Another silence.

"Where are you now?"

"Tampa. I'm in a motel here."

"Alone?"

"Yes, alone. God. A man is the last thing I need right now."

Lexie chuckled. "Okay. Give me a minute and let me call you back."

The second the call disconnected, Jen worried that she'd made a mistake. She and Lexie had been friendly the whole time she was in St. Thomas, but that didn't necessarily mean they were friends. What if Lexie decided to do a little digging and found the articles about the museum and the missing pieces? What if she—

Stop it. Wait to see what she has to say.

She paced the floor of the motel room, chewing her

lip and raking her fingers through her hair while she waited for Lexie to call her back. She vacillated between wondering if she could trust Lexie and worrying that she'd made a mistake drawing her into this situation. But then, it wasn't as if she had a bunch of choices. When the phone rang at last, she almost jumped out of her skin.

"Lexie?"

"Unless you gave this number to a bunch of people."

Jen swallowed a hysterical laugh. "Not a chance."

"Okay, write down this number." She recited one to Jen. "When we hang up, call him. He's a friend of mine who's a pilot with his own small plane. As a matter of fact, he lives in one of those communities where people keep their plane at their houses and use a common runaway."

"Are you kidding me?"

"Not in the least. Anyway, he owes me a big favor. He'll tell you how to connect with him. He's going to fly you to Hermosa."

"What?" Her jaw dropped. "But what—I mean—"

"I could tell you were really stressed and needed some help. You'll owe me big time, Jen, and one of these days, I'll collect. But what will you do with your car?"

"I, uh, thought I'd sell it if I managed to get to the Caribbean. Find another good used one when I got there?"

"Oh, right. Smart move. That's what some people do when they relocate like this. I could help you find one."

"You're being so nice to me." Jen wondered what

the catch was.

She could hear Lexie's sigh all the way across the connection. "When I left St. Thomas, it wasn't the best situation for me. I'll tell you about it someday. And I got help when I least expected it. I like to think I'm paying it forward. Besides, you were always good to me. I'm happy to help."

Thank god! Talk about luck.

"Well, I'll take it. Thank you."

"Meanwhile, call that number," Lexie urged, "and ask for Mark. He's expecting you."

"I can't believe you just did this for me. I don't know how to thank you."

"You just did. Call Mark. Get your car sold. Grab a cab to where he hangars his plane. I'll see you this afternoon. And Jen? It's okay. It's my turn to do something nice for you."

Jen just stared at the phone when Lexie hung up. What the hell? She hoped this wasn't some big joke the woman was playing on her. Crossing her fingers, she dialed the number. And hoped she could stay invisible until she got to Hermosa.

Chapter Seven

Roger Welborn poured two inches of very old Scotch into a cut crystal rocks glass, added three ice cubes, and leaned back in his chair. It wasn't even five o'clock yet, and normally, he limited himself to one drink until the sun went down. But normally, he wasn't consumed with frustration and anger over a problem he couldn't seem to get a handle on.

He took a swallow of the Scotch, letting it slide down his tongue. Then he looked at the man across from him. "Fuck."

Peter Leneghan nodded. "I agree."

"You do?" Welborn sat forward in his chair. "Then why the hell aren't you doing more about our problem? Where is that fucking bitch?"

"We're looking," the other man assured him. "I have men on it. Believe me."

"Look harder. I want those missing pieces. All of them, including the ones that were earmarked for the museum. I want Sutherland's ass on a skewer. And I want the LaCroix woman dead. Right now, no one knows I have a connection to this. If my role in this drama ever gets out, I'm finished."

"Roger. Please. I'm well aware of that. I have every feeler out." Leneghan walked over to the bar in Welborn's den and poured his own drink. Then he turned to face Roger. "The man is like a ghost. He had to have planned this for a very long time, at least according to the very large size of his gambling debt."

"What I'd like to know," Welborn growled, "is how he set this up. You know he has another buyer. He's so in debt he can't afford to blow me off unless he's got someone offering a higher price. Someone willing to buy the entire shipment. I want to know how he made his plans, found the right off-the-books buyer, and managed to make both himself and all those missing pieces disappear without a trace."

"I'm telling you, I'm reaching out to everyone everywhere for even the slightest smell of this."

"And how did the woman get involved in it? She wasn't part of anything at the beginning."

"That we know of," Leneghan said. "All you have is Sutherland's word that she got her hands on the goods and screwed him out of them. Just whatever he told you in that last conversation."

Yeah, the conversation. Because he knew what a mess things were at the museum, and because Sutherland wouldn't meet him with the latest artifacts. Of course not. And where the hell was the main shipment for the museum, anyway? How had it all just disappeared?

The weenie tried to tell him on the phone that Jen LaCroix had the stuff, but he believed that about as much as he believed in Santa Claus. Still, he couldn't rule it out, which was why he had people scouring the globe for the woman. Then, after the piece of shit lied to him, he'd hung up on him, and now he was in the wind. Welborn knew he should have gone to the museum to confront Sutherland, but that was the last place he wanted this stuff aired out. He was hung either way.

"Here's another theory," Leneghan went on. "What if he set this up with the LaCroix bitch way in advance? What if this is all an act and they both disappear so the missing pieces can't be tracked? And they sell them somewhere for a pile of money and disappear forever?"

"Sutherland and LaCroix?" Welborn shook his head. "I don't see them together. Yes, I know I could be misreading this, but I've spent enough time with both of them. They aren't together. I'd have smelled it out long before this. They aren't good enough to hide it from me."

"Okay, try this," Leneghan continued. "We don't even know if she was really involved, or a red herring Sutherland tossed your way. Maybe he just threw her into this to get you and the Feds chasing someone other than him."

Welborn shook his head. "Doesn't matter. It's not that I totally believe what Sutherland said, but I have to find her on the off chance she has a real connection. I want those fucking antiquities. I don't care if someone offered him twice what I'm paying. We had an ongoing deal, so I fucking want them. Otherwise, he's a dead man. I need to send a message about what happens to people who screw with me."

"Who knew you had this deal going with him?"

Welborn frowned. "I didn't think anyone did. And very few people have ever been invited into the locked, private room where I keep my antiquities collection. Damn!"

They drank for a moment in silence.

"How many people do we have on this?" he asked at last.

"Ten. Obviously not enough." Leneghan shook his head. "You're right. We have to find that damn woman. She could be the key to all of this. If it turns out she isn't, we need to get rid of her and get back on the trail of those artifacts immediately."

"It's probably just a pile of shit to mislead me," Welborn pointed out, "but she might know who the buyer is. She worked with Sutherland for ten years."

Leneghan nodded. "It's possible, but why throw her to the wolves like he did?"

"Misdirection." Welborn ground his teeth. "Damn it, she seemed like such a nobody. Not at all someone who would be mixed up this kind of shit. I hardly ever misjudge people like this."

"If it's any consolation," Leneghan told him, "she never impressed me that way either, the few times I was around her. Just a plain, conservative broad who worked at the museum and lived a very private life. Always in the background, quietly doing her job. I believe she has a kid but no husband."

Welborn grunted. "Then I'd like to know how the hell she found out what was going on and stuck herself into it."

"We don't even know for sure that she did," Leneghan pointed out. "We're just taking the word of a rat for it, a rat trying to throw suspicion on someone else. Like I said before, muddy the waters."

Welborn took another sip of his drink. "Another reason to accelerate your search for her. Either nab her or write her off. Every minute that passes is another minute farther away from those artifacts. Find the woman, get the artifacts if she has them, then kill her."

"What if she really doesn't have them?"

"Kill her anyway. We can't leave people who can talk."

He knew he was irritating Leneghan, but damn it, he was royally pissed off himself. Everything had turned to shit. He ground his teeth. The man had been with him for ten years and was paid an obscene amount of money to do the dirty work. He was sure that was the only thing that kept Leneghan's temper in check, but his own temper was skating on the edge.

He had dropped the ball on this as much as everyone else and that aggravated him even more. He was so sure he had Craig Sutherland by the balls, keeping in touch with the man and monitoring his life. When he'd first spotted him in a high-stakes poker game in a private room at one of the local casinos, he'd seen a way to get the man under his control and coerce him into smuggling antiquities into the country for him. Inviting him to his private poker game had been the first step. The other players had been a little curious, but it made sense that the chairman of the museum board would invite the director if he gambled. Then he'd manipulated the situation, so Sutherland won only enough to keep him coming but lost enough to need a way to pay off his debt.

For the past four years the relationship had been successful, at least as far as Welborn was concerned. Why had it all fallen apart?

He wasn't a man given to uncontrolled rage, but his blood boiled at this situation. It was his fault, his own stupidity that caused him to miss the delivery date of the latest shipment. He'd trusted Sutherland to give him the correct information. Big mistake. When Sutherland notified him the entire shipment had arrived two days early and had disappeared, he was enraged both personally and as the chair of the museum board. It never occurred to him that the man would double cross him and decide to keep it all for himself. He wanted to wring someone's neck, preferably Sutherland's.

Fuck and double fuck.

"You know we're checking the LaCroix woman's history since she landed in Michigan ten years ago," Leneghan reminded him. "We're following the connection to anyone whose name shows up. Just in case. But who the hell could have expected this? She was just a name on the employee list all this time. Nothing that stood out."

"We don't know that now," Welborn pointed out. "You need to dig back in her history and find out every single thing about her you can. And I mean everything. There has to be something we're missing."

He wasn't used to having things like that happen in his projects.

"And go back to questioning those people from the museum but quietly." Welborn gave him a hard stare. "Find out who she was friends with and focus on them."

The muscle twitched in Leneghan's face. The man wasn't used to being interrogated this way. Of course he seldom had to do it. The two of them had been together many, many years, and he'd never failed once. But Welborn really wanted those artifacts in a big way. They were his and that was that.

"At the risk of repeating myself," he said, "since we can't find a smell of either Sutherland or the woman anywhere, we keep your people on them. But also sniff around and see if maybe someone else was doing a deal with him. I'd like to think that's not the case, but we can't overlook anything."

"You think it might be another player from the card game?"

"I'd say anything is possible, damn it. Where else would he connect with someone that has that kind of money and could also get his dick in a wringer? We have to find out who it is if that's what happened."

Leneghan nodded. "We'll be all over it, but quietly."

"Yes. Find him. Or her." Welborn downed the rest of his drink. "This means he or she probably knows about me, and that's a problem. What is equally as important here is to send a signal to whoever thinks about stepping into my territory that there is a severe penalty."

"Agreed." Leneghan finished his drink, rose from his chair, and set his empty glass on the bar. "I'll get right on it."

"Do that," Welborn told him. "And keep on the hunt to find that goddamned female. She has to know something. She's off the grid, and I want her found."

Leneghan nodded. "I'll be in touch shortly."

"See that you are."

Welborn watched the man leave, keeping his anger under control only because he'd trained himself to do it for years. Collecting these rare artifacts was the single most satisfying element of his life. The women in his life had finally blended so he could hardly tell one from another. He still got a high from screwing people on business deals, because it reinforced his belief that he was smarter than everyone else.

But the real orgasm came from illegally buying rare artifacts. He had a special section of his house, tastefully decorated and secure from the rest of the place, where he could sit and admire them for hours. Sometimes he took one of his women in there and told her the history of one while he fucked her brains out. It always made the orgasm more intense.

And now, that asshole Sutherland was fucking it all up. Well, not if he had anything to say about it. He'd find the artifacts and then make sure everyone who had anything to do with this shitstorm never fucked with him again. Leneghan was as good as they came. That was why he'd been a part of this team for as long as he had. But sometimes there was a different tack to take.

He might just be able to get a lead on Jennifer LaCroix faster than Leneghan. He pulled out his cell phone, scrolled through his contacts and found the number he wanted.

"Yeah," he said when the call was answered. "I have an assignment for you. Interested?"

****

Dino loved lying in bed with Jen, feeling her body next to his. The feel of her next to him was more electric than with any other woman, ever.

"Your skin is so soft. Just like the rest of you," he whispered against the delicate skin of her ear. He could feel the tremors it sent through her body.

"I love the feel of your solid muscles against me." Her words were like a caress.

"Yeah?" He trailed his fingers down her spine.

"Uh huh. Your chest is so solid." She giggled. "Along with other parts of your body."

A shiver skittered over him as she stroked the flat

planes of his muscular chest, his long legs, his thick cock nestled between her thighs and nudging against her sex.

"And you're so…hard," she teased,

"And getting harder." He pressed his cock against her and shifted his hips suggestively.

"Maybe we should do something about that."

"Maybe we should. Got any ideas?"

"I might. Let me show you." She pushed upward on his shoulders, lightly, but it was enough to make him turn over and lie on his back.

"I'm all yours, *querida*."

She kissed the flat plane of his stomach then licked the spot. "And don't you forget it."

"No worries," he breathed as his cock flexed.

"Lift your arms and grab the headboard," she ordered. "I don't want you interfering with my playtime."

He huffed a laugh. "Playtime, is it? I love playtime. With you."

Obediently, he reached back and grabbed two of the spindles in the headboard and gripped them hard. He was torn between wanting to give himself over to her completely and throwing her on her back so he could taste every inch of her.

She smoothed a hand over his chest before closing her teeth over one flat nipple.

Oh, Jesus! He nearly came right then and there.

That was the thing with Jen. He'd had great sex with more women than he could count, but with her, all they had to do was touch each other and they exploded. When she bit down, he couldn't stop the low moan that rumbled from his throat.

"Damn, Jen. You just completely undo me. Do that again."

Her laugh was low and soft. "You like my teeth on you?"

"I like your everything on me."

And that was no lie. Her touch was head and shoulders above that of any other woman he'd ever been with. In fact, if he was truly honest, she made memories of every other woman disappear from his life altogether. What did that mean? Did he have the guts to try and build a future with her? Committing to one woman scared the shit out of him, but Jen LaCroix was not like other women. She brought a magic into his life that both tantalized and frightened him. He'd been a loner for so long. Could he take a chance here?

The soft lick of her tongue sent a shaft of heat directly to his cock. His arms jerked as he forced himself to keep his fingers gripping the headboard.

She paid so much attention to one nipple it nearly made him come. But then she looked up at him, gave him one of her sexy smiles, and shifted her concentration to the next one. She tugged it with her teeth and gave it a gentle bite. He would have told her to keep doing that forever, but other areas of his body were demanding her attention.

She moved her mouth slowly down his body, taking tiny nips then soothing them with her tongue. She grinned at the sounds of pleasure that exploded from his mouth as he became more and more aroused. He nearly levitated off the bed when she sifted her fingers through the hair surrounding his cock before gripping the hard, thick shaft and slowly stroking it up and down. The faster she stroked the choppier his breathing became and the more his heart rate accelerated.

"Faster," he told her. "Harder."

Oh, sweet Jesus. He was sure his cock was going to explode. Her touch always seemed to set his motor on fast forward the way no other woman ever had.

She extended her tongue to lick the entire length of him, up one side and down the other. Then she did it again before tightening her fingers on him and beginning that up and down glide that got him so hot. When she probed the opening at the tip of the head, he had to grit his teeth to hold on.

As she stroked faster and licked more thoroughly, Dino yanked his hands from the headboard. He had to touch her. Had to. He slipped one hand down over the swell of her hip and the curve of her ass to that hot cleft between the cheeks. When she sucked harder and stroked faster, he probed the hot cleft until he found the sensitive opening he was looking for and teased it with his fingers.

She rocked herself on his hand, even as she continued to speed up the strokes on his cock.

Harder.

Faster.

More, more, more.

And then he exploded, his muscles twitching as he spurted into her mouth.

His body jerked with each spasm, his heart pounding and his breath seesawing in and out of his lungs. It seemed to go on forever until finally it slowed, and his muscles began to relax. When his heart rate returned somewhat to normal, he opened his eyes and—

Dino jerked awake, his hand, not Jen's, wrapped

around his still pulsing cock.

Great.

He'd just given himself another hand job, which seemed to be his normal fallback activity since Jen had disappeared.

Fucking damn.

He got out of bed very quietly and made his way to the bathroom to clean up. The last thing he needed was Ethan waking up and asking him what the hell was going on.

Van Dine had not called him back yet, but he wasn't surprised. A man who was plugged into as many black situations as he was, who was on so many people's shit list because of it, never called back the first time. Right now, Dino was sure the man was checking all his dark contacts to see if Dino was setting some kind of trap for him. As soon as it was light, Dino would put in another call. There wasn't time to waste.

He slept fitfully the remainder of the night, finally giving up the ghost at six thirty and putting on a pot of coffee. He'd toyed with the idea of getting a single serving coffee maker, but as he liked to tell people, he was an old dog who didn't want to learn new tricks. There was just something about the flavor of real brewed coffee that couldn't be duplicated. When it was ready, he filled a big mug and took it, along with his cell phone, out to the front porch. The view from there allowed him to watch the sunrise, which gave him a feeling of peace he badly needed.

Yesterday, after they'd arrived back at the house, he and Ethan had both spent time reaching out to people they thought could help locate Jen, although he had a feeling Martin Van Dine was his best hope. He was pissed off at himself that he hadn't ever bothered to know the names of people she was friendly with while they were together. Actually, he was pissed off at himself for a lot of reasons. He'd taken for granted a woman who, in retrospect, had brightened his life and brought him joy and pleasure without asking anything in return. He was so busy being the dark ops agent, unfettered and reveling in the danger, that he hadn't for a minute stopped to realize the treasure he had.

Last night, he'd reached out to people he'd known when he was in and out of St. Thomas, thinking it was a good thing he had a habit of keeping people's numbers. Some of them, of course, were no longer in existence, which he expected. Some, he'd had to leave a message for. The two people he did reach said they hadn't seen or heard from Jen since she'd left so suddenly and wanted to know why he was looking for her after all this time.

Finally, he pulled up the number for Martin Van Dine. Sometimes it took three or four calls before Dino connected with him. Van Dine skated on the thin edge of legitimacy and was always on someone's shit list. Only the fact that he had amassed what amounted to ten small fortunes and could protect himself six ways from Sunday kept him alive.

A click sounded and then a recorded message came on.

"You probably called this number by mistake. You can leave a message, but there's no guarantee you'll get a callback."

Another click.

"Listen, asshole, it's Dino Brancuzzi, the man who saved your worthless life in the worst shitstorm we could imagine. You said you'd pay me back one day. Well, today is that day. Call me. ASAP."

He disconnected, swallowed the last of the coffee, then sat staring off into the sunrise.

"Okay." Ethan, who had been sitting at the kitchen table, stood up. "I've hung out here long enough waiting to see if you made contact. Whatever else she is, Jen is good at staying invisible. I made some calls last night and got nowhere. I was hoping to get a hint of where she'd disappeared before I left here so we could get this search rolling. But damn it, she's just erased herself."

Dino raked his fingers though his hair. "Tell me about it."

"I've gotta get moving. If indeed she's in the Caribbean as you think, there's a zillion little islands she could be tucked away on. And nobody on them would have any idea of her situation unless she told them, which I hardly think she will. So I was hoping we could cut out a trip to the frozen north and both of us jump right into the search. But it looks like I need to haul ass up there and snag my sources."

"That apparently is not the case." Dino rose from his chair and opened the front screen door. "Yes, you do. But breakfast first while we make a list of possible locations. I can work those while you shake your sources and try to locate the missing pieces and who has them. And why."

"So how about this? Let's go inside, and I'll fix some breakfast while we make a list of possible locations. The smaller and more remote the better."

"Fine," Ethan said, "as long as we get right to it. I'll put up the list while you cook. I see you still have that whiteboard on your kitchen wall."

Dino chuckled. "Still using it, as a matter of fact."

In the years after Dino moved to Key West and began taking "private" charters, he'd incorporated habits from CIA missions into his personal activity. One of his staples was a white board on his kitchen wall where he could both make notations and paste notes. He handed Ethan a marking pen and a map of the Caribbean that he'd placed on the table the night before.

"Okay. Get to it. We'll analyze the list while we eat."

By the time Dino brought plates of scrambled eggs, bacon, and tropical fruit to the table and refilled the coffee mugs, they'd created a list of every island that seemed likely and marked them on the map.

"Let's start with the second tier," Ethan suggested, "and work our way down to the lowest. We can look for possible places where she can work as well as live. I have no idea of her financial situation."

They had finished breakfast, shoved their plates aside, and were halfway down the list when Dino's phone rang. He looked at the readout. Well, hell. Martin Van Dine actually was calling him back.

"I thought there was a good chance you were dead," he said by way of greeting.

"I think a lot of people would be very happy if I was." The man's rough, rusty-sounding voice hadn't changed a bit.

"If you can give me some answers, I'll sure be happy that you're not."

"It's been a long time since you reached out," Van Dine commented. "You must really have your dick in a wringer this time."

"More or less." Although he could think of a much better place he'd rather put it. "I'm looking for someone."

"Must be someone damn important for you to chase me down."

Dino frowned. How to explain this without Van Dine giving him ten kinds of shit about it? Tell the truth. There'd been enough lying already in this shitstorm.

"Yes, she is. No editorial comment, okay?"

There was a moment of silence, then Van Dine's rough laugh echoed across the connection.

"Don't tell me Mister Hot Dick, the great Dino Brancuzzi, has finally bitten the dust."

"I'm hoping it just didn't happen too late."

Van Dine barked a laugh. "I won't even ask you what that means. So what can I do for you?"

Dino swallowed back his impatience. He was fortunate Van Dine had called him back at all. "I'm trying to pinpoint a place where a woman alone would go to hide herself from a variety of people hunting for her."

"Nothing's ever simple with you, is it?"

"Apparently not. And there's one other piece of this puzzle." He paused. "I need to find out who runs a high-stakes private poker game in the Detroit area and who the players are."

"Damn! Fuck me blind. You don't want much, do you?"

Dino swallowed a sigh. "I need this info, and I need it yesterday. You've got contacts out there. I'm going to do my own looking, but you can get into corners I can't. Something definitely shady is going on here, and I'm not too proud to ask for help."

"Yeah? That seems to be a regular thing with you. What's the urgency this time?"

Dino swallowed a sigh. "Okay, here's the deal."

He related the situation in short, concise sentences, all about Welborn, Sutherland, and how Jen was caught in the net. He didn't have to embroider anything with Van Dine.

"Are you shitting me? Welborn's supposed to be some rich social bigwig. How did he get into something like this?"

"The more money you have," Dino reminded the man, "the more you think laws don't apply to you. You know that."

"Yeah, well, it's unfortunate that your woman is somehow in their line of sight."

Dino swallowed the sharp taste that surged into his mouth. Hearing Van Dine voice the situation made his stomach knot. He had to find Jen before these people did, or she was as good as dead.

"Okay. Shoot me a picture of her, and message me the names of everyone involved. I'll put some feelers out. I'll see if a single female has shown up lately."

"How the hell would you find that out?" Dino asked.

"Trade secret. People tell me things. And please, on your end, do your best to stay as low-level as possible."

"I hear you," Dino told him, "but you know I'm not gonna sit around on my thumbs. First, it's not my style and second, she's in a lot of danger."

"Do you know anyone who isn't?" Van Dine joked. "Okay. Look at a map and let's exchange our ideas on possible places Jen could be hiding. I know you can hunt with the best, but—"

"But you can find out things I can't," Dino agreed. "As soon as we hang up, I'll send you Jen's picture plus the names of the other people I'm after. And I'll send you the list of islands I'm going to hit myself. The other side of the coin is finding out where Sutherland has managed to hide himself."

"Send me what you've got, and I'll get started."

Dino disconnected the call and turned back to Ethan.

"So we're going hunting," his friend said. "I'll head up north to start digging."

"Yeah. Let's hope Van Dine can help us narrow down the search parameters."

For a man whose life was the dangerous work he did and who swore he'd never be tied down, this was a real wakeup call. Apparently, it had taken a disaster to shock him into realizing he'd let the best thing in his life walk away from him. And he was still trying to come to terms with it. He knew time was running out, and he had to move fast.

****

It was early afternoon when the small plane landed at the Hermosa airport. Mark Ballentine had been friendly and efficient and willing to help a friend of Lexie's. He didn't even hesitate when she told him she was carrying a small firearm. Apparently, that was nothing new for him.

"Customs is used to checking my passengers on the plane, so they don't have to stand in line. We'll take care of it."

And he did. The customs agent who boarded the

plane interviewed her with a pleasant manner, made a cursory check of her suitcases, and shook her hand. "Welcome to Hermosa. Mr. Ballentine's passengers are always welcome. Enjoy your stay."

As soon as he was gone, Ballentine helped her move her gun from the suitcase to an inside pocket in her purse, then preceded her down the drop out stairs. She grabbed her sunglasses from her purse to shield her eyes from the dazzling light.

Mark Ballentine grinned. "It's definitely bright."

"I keep forgetting just how intense it is in this part of the world."

Standing in the bright, blazing sun, she realized that after living in Michigan for ten years she didn't remember how hot and humid it was in the Caribbean. The truth was, though, right now she needed to be someplace she was familiar with and where she had contacts. Where she could hide and people would keep her secret and not betray her.

Where she could feel safe if that was possible.

Mark jogged down the stairway and held out his hand. "Thanks for flying Ballentine Air."

"Are you kidding? Thank you for doing this. I don't know what else I would have done."

"Lexie gets all the thanks. She seems to be really good at pulling strings to help people."

Jen cocked her head and studied his face. "I sense a story there. She wouldn't tell me why you agreed to this, and I'm guessing you won't either."

She'd been so anxious to get out of Tampa and into the Caribbean without worrying about Customs or any other possible trap, she hadn't bothered to ask. Her entire focus had been on watching for someone trailing her or spotting her, although she had no idea how she'd recognize that.

He shrugged. "We all have our secrets. "Let me get your stuff."

While she waited for her luggage, she looked around the tarmac. The Hermosa airport was definitely ten steps down from the ones she was used to. From what she could tell, they'd landed on the only runaway, and there were only two other planes at rest on the tarmac, both small for the larger commercial airlines and neither of which she'd ever heard of. Just how off the grid was this place, anyway?

She couldn't help scanning the few people still disembarking but nothing raised a red flag. She didn't get that feeling creeping up her spine that had been happening lately.

Mark opened the plane's cargo hold, pulled out the two bags she'd taken with her, and rolled them over to her.

"Thanks for everything," she told him. "I mean it."

"Good luck with whatever is going on." He nodded toward the small terminal. "And there's Lexie waiting for you."

Jen looked over toward the building. Sure enough, Lexie was waving at her as she hurried across the tarmac, looking just as Jen remembered with her thick blonde hair pulled back in a ponytail and her curvy body clad in knee-length shorts and a colorful T-shirt. Jen always liked to call her Miss Caribbean. Sun glinted off her colorful dangling earrings.

Jen took a moment to scan the area again, although she wasn't sure what she expected to see. Thugs with guns rushing toward her?

Ridiculous.

Taking a deep breath, she hurried over to the terminal building, pulling her bags behind her.

"First a hug," Lexie said, wrapping her arms around her. "I know we haven't seen each other in ages and even though we weren't best friends, we were good friends. And everyone needs a hug now and then, including me."

Boy! Wasn't that just the truth?

"Listen." Jen hugged her back." You are probably my only friend right now, and I'm happy to give you all the hugs you want."

Lexie eyed her up and down. "Even in trouble, you still look great. Come on, let's get you out of here."

She took one of the suitcases, and Jen took the others, scanning the people just arriving and those in the small terminal. Did anyone seem out of place? How could she even tell? Anyway, how would Welborn or anyone else know she was here? She hadn't even known Hermosa existed until she got in touch with Lexie.

Still, she tried to look everywhere as they moved through the terminal to the curb where Lexie's car was parked.

"The pleasures of a small airport," Lexie told her. "You can park right by the front door."

"I'm guessing no major airlines fly in here?" Jen looked at the crowd exiting the terminal, again trying to see if someone rang a bell. Only how would she know? And would Welborn fly commercial if he came here? He probably had his own plane or a friend with one who'd loan it to him.

Lexie nodded. "Not commercial. He'd want his

own schedule and control of his transportation. And there are more private planes than commercial, and no big ones. The people who live here like it that way. The people who come here are very ordinary and low key. Business is good, life is good, and they're happy."

"Good. That means…" She paused.

Lexie glanced over at her. "That whoever you're running from isn't going to make this the first place they look. Or even the tenth."

"What?" Her body tensed. Did Lexie know something?

"Please. I'm not stupid. I know all the signs. I wasn't born yesterday. Besides, people other than tourists don't come to stay on Hermosa unless they need to get away from something. Or someone. I always liked you, Jen, and we always got along well. Now, I'm just glad I can help you, even in a small way."

"This is much more than small," Jen assured her. "I probably shouldn't even involve you in this. I didn't think I might be putting you in danger. I only—"

Lexie held up a hand. "It's okay. I didn't think this was just a bad breakup. You can tell me as much or as little as you want. But first, let's get out of here."

She pulled away from the curb and headed out of the airport.

"I didn't even think about a place to stay." Jen realized she'd overlooked too many things in her haste to get as far away as possible. "Can I get a room at the hotel? Is it expensive? Is there such a thing as rooming houses here?"

"Maybe. And the hotel is pretty full, but no need to spend money. I've got a nice little two-bedroom apartment. Nothing fancy, but it's clean and has a great view. And I'd love to have a roommate."

"Oh, no," she protested. "I can't do that. Besides imposing on you, I hate that I'm already dragging you into my mess. I don't—"

"Stop." Lexie reached over and put her hand on Jen's arm. "You can relax here. It's highly unlikely that anyone can trace you to this place. I don't care who they are. We're off the beaten path and hardly on anyone's radar. Hermosa is a vacation spot for people on a budget." She glanced over at Jen. "Besides, it will be fun to have a roommate for a while. The dive shop job doesn't pay all that much, so you don't need to be blowing money on a hotel room. If it works for you, your share of the rent won't be much."

"I…" She swallowed. "Thank you, Lexie. This is above and beyond. Just tell me what my share of the rent is. I…have some money, and I don't freeload, especially not on someone who's helping me out the way you have." She bit her lip. "I hope I don't end up bringing trouble to your doorstep. I guess all I thought about was getting out of the States and finding someplace, um, innocuous."

"Listen, it was obvious you were hauling some kind of trouble around with you. Remember, I could have said no." For a moment Lexie was silent. "You know you can tell me whatever's chasing you. I can keep my mouth shut."

But not about this.

"For which I am very grateful. Thank you."

Lexie shrugged. "Okay, but if you need to unload, you should remember shit just rolls off my shoulders."

You don't want any part of this, believe me.

Jen watched the scenery unwind as they drove through the town. Colorful buildings dotted the streets, most of them in Spanish style architecture, and watching out the window Jen got a sense the place was very much like St. Thomas, typical Caribbean. She could actually hear the salt water lapping at the shore and smell it. Too bad she couldn't relax and enjoy it. But ever since she'd left the house in Michigan, her stomach had been tied in knots and tension gripped her entire body like a constant companion.

She tried to glance at the sideview mirror as casually as she could, then realized she had no idea what she was looking for. Anyway, the chances he even knew about this place were slim to none. If nothing else, she'd bought herself some breathing room.

Had she made a mistake coming here? The place was just as tiny as it looked on the map. She'd really have to scope it out for options in case she had to make a quick exit. There weren't many places to hide in a small island country like this. She also reminded herself that anyone arriving at the island would be known to the population before they settled in and that was a benefit.

Lexie made a left turn onto a street that ran beside the Caribbean Sea and another one into a parking lot.

"Here we are."

A three-story building painted a soft tropical blue faced the water. Attractive tropical landscaping took away the severity of the building and made it look welcoming.

Jen just stared. "What a great location."

"I know, right? There's a big pool in the back," Lexie told her, "but the beach is right across the street, and I prefer that."

"Lexie, this must cost a fortune."

Lexie shook her head. "Believe it or not, it's very reasonable. The couple that owns it came here many years ago broke and looking for a place to put down roots and raise a family. I guess a lot of people helped them, so they say they're just paying it forward."

I couldn't have picked a better place to hide.

Lexie hauled one of the suitcases out of the trunk. "Let's get you inside and unpacked. Then, it's still early enough that I can take you down to the dive shop and introduce you to Matt and Clay."

Jen giggled. She couldn't help herself, and it was nice to laugh for a moment.

"Did they make those names up? They're perfect for divers."

Lexie grinned. "No, but they do fit."

"Then let's just dump my stuff. I can unpack later. I want to meet them and see if this will work."

She kept looking over her shoulder and all around her as they hauled her luggage into the second-floor apartment, but nothing made her shoulders itch. And thankfully Lexie didn't comment. If this job really worked out, maybe when this was all over, she could bring Deanne down here and they could make a nice, stress-free life for themselves.

Except of course there was Dino, who was now in their lives. How would she handle that?

Chapter Eight

Jen and Lexie unloaded Jen's suitcases, and Lexie showed her around the apartment. It was small but more than sufficient, and airy, with high ceilings and lots of windows. After that, Lexie drove her to The Dive Shop, which was really its name, to meet the owners, Matt and Clay.

The marina was small but very busy. No cruise ships. Jen figured the island was too small and unexciting for them to schedule stops there. There were several private boats moored along the three docks. It was an interesting mix of commercial fishing boats, pleasure boats, dive boats, and whatever. They were familiar to her after all the time she'd spent on St. Thomas.

If she got this job, there was both a positive and a negative side to it. On one hand, if whoever the man behind all this somehow managed to track her here, she was out in the open where she could easily be spotted. On the other hand, she'd be able to see them when they pulled into the marina and get herself out of sight. It was a two-edged sword that she had to wield carefully, assuming they even heard of this place.

She followed Jen as she walked to The Dive Shop located right at the beginning of the dock. Two men a little younger than she was and who she guessed were the owners were tying off a boat in the first berth. They helped a couple climb from the boat to the dock, shook hands with them, and the happy tourists headed toward the parking lot. It looked as if they'd just returned from an excursion. The owners were young, good looking, and from what they said, desperate to find someone to run the business side of things while they gave lessons and led diving excursions.

"That's our focus," Matt told her. "And we're very good at it."

"But we suck at running a business," Clay added, grinning.

The figure they named for her salary would have been embarrassing on St. Thomas, but Jen gathered everything was less on Hermosa. Besides, she had the stash she'd been saving since she got to Michigan. Plenty of cash with her and a nice round sum waiting in the bank for when it was safe to tap into it again. And no one could find her here. She hoped.

She tried not to be obvious as she kept checking the dock and the area around it while they were talking to her. An hour later, she'd seen everything they could show her about the dive shop, which wasn't much. She could work the cash register, had a price list of the inventory, and had learned the rudiments of the business. She was comfortable she could do it in her sleep.

"So tomorrow?" Matt asked, a hopeful look on his face.

"Or even today?" Clay grinned.

"Tomorrow," Lexie said. "Don't push."

"Oh, and you get free T-shirts," Clay grinned. "One of the perks."

"Really, it's because wearing it advertises the

shop," Matt added.

Jen took the pile of shirts from them, thanked them, shook hands, and said she'd see them in the morning.

"Is there a place here that has cheap used cars?" she asked Lexie.

"Oh, sure." Lexie nodded. "I know the owner. I can get you a good deal."

Jen laughed. "Do you know everyone here?"

Lexie winked. "There aren't that many people to know. Okay, let's get you some wheels."

As they drove from the dock through the town to the dealership, Jen realized there was hardly a place more low key than this for her to bury herself. She could be Plain Jen, in old cutoffs, a dive shop T-shirt, and no makeup. No one would recognize her unless they looked very hard.

Assuming, of course, they could even find her here first, and that was long odds. She was pretty sure a microscope would be needed to find Hermosa. Even if they heard about it, they'd dismiss it as a place to search for her. Still, she couldn't help being extra alert as Lexie drove them through the streets of the little town, studying people, trying to decide if the tourists were really tourists.

One thing was a given. Whoever Sutherland had been originally selling the goods to was not going to let the loss of the artifacts he'd been expecting go lightly. If it was Welborn, there would be nineteen kinds of hell to pay. The FBI probably had a full team on this by now. And the museum board certainly would be all over the missing items that were supposed to go to them. What had they thought about her sudden disappearance? Did they really think she was part of this scheme with Craig? Or by herself? How had her nice, quiet, boring life turned into such a disaster?

She wondered how Dino had reacted at his first contact with Deanne. And how her daughter felt about Dino. If she made it out of this alive, she knew she had ten years to make up for to both of them.

"Those must be some heavy thoughts." Lexie's voice broke into her mental ramblings.

"Just thinking about...stuff."

"Stuff," Lexie repeated. "Okay. But I could probably help you better if I knew what sent you running to this almost invisible little island."

"Thank you for that, but I don't think you want to get involved in my mess. I'm just so grateful you offered me this situation without asking any questions."

"No sweat. Now. I can take you to the place where I bought my car, but Jen? Do you really think you need one? This island is very small, they have a great bus system, and I can take you just about any place you need to go. And if you're trying to stay off the radar, which I'm sure is why you came here to Noplace, that's just one more traceable item."

Jen nibbled on her lower lip. Lexie was making sense, but... "I don't want to keep imposing on you. And what if I need to go someplace and you're working or something?"

Lexie's forehead creased in a brief frown. "Okay. How about this? I'll take you whenever I can, other times there's the bus. If I'm not using my car, you can borrow, and we'll split expenses."

Jen had to admit it made sense. Buying a car would leave a footprint for someone to stumble over, and really, like Lexie said, there were other options.

Besides, if she had to leave here in a hurry, it would mean just leaving the car or trying to sell it fast. "Okay."

She grinned and turned back toward the apartment. "I always said you were smart."

Jen hoped so. She couldn't lie to herself. Roger Welborn had to be ready to carve people up by this time. Not being able to reach any of the people involved had to be driving him insane. She was glad that Deanne was safe at Ethan's where none of these maniacs could get at her and harm her or use her for leverage.

But she couldn't stay here forever. She had to take a chance on a call from one of her burner phones. Calling Ethan should be safe. He had more security than the president.

"I need to make a couple of phone calls," she told Lexie. "Can you pull over and give me a few minutes?"

"You can have all the minutes you want. You've been on the go all day. When we get home, you can have a shower, unpack, and we can grab some dinner."

"Don't you have to work?" Jen asked.

"Yes, but my boss graciously gave me today off for personal business." She grinned. "He's great to work for. You have the address?" When Jen nodded, she said, "Okay, meet you there."

"Good."

Lexie found a place on a side street to park. Jen got out of the car, pulled out one of her phones, and dialed Ethan's cell number, which she had memorized.

"Where the hell are you?" he growled. "Everyone's half nuts wondering if you're okay."

"I'm sorry, but I can't tell you. It's better if you

don't know. That way everyone's safe."

"Are you fucking kidding me? No one's safe at the moment, including you. Dino's—"

"I just wanted to make sure Deanne was okay," she interrupted. "Can I talk to her?"

"You could if I was home, which I'm not."

Oh, god. If he wasn't there, who was protecting Lisa and Jamie and most of all Deanne?

"You mean everyone is unprotected? Ethan, I brought Deanne there, because I knew she'd be safe with you. If you—"

"Hold it. Take a breath, okay? Guardian Security has their best teams at the house on twenty-four/seven guard duty. Everyone's fine. Do you think I'd leave them with no protection? Shit, Jen."

"Sorry, sorry, sorry. Just…nervous." About everything.

"And with good reason. You have some ugly people after you. But let's set your mind at ease on this. Deanne's fine. I just checked in with Lisa and with Guardian fifteen minutes ago."

She let out the breath she'd been holding. "Thank you. Thank you."

"Jen, Dino's combing the Caribbean looking for you. He's half out of his mind with worry. You have to let him know where you are so he can protect you."

"Protect me?" She wanted to laugh. "Why? He hasn't even seen me for ten years. Never even made an effort to find me."

"Do you know that for sure?"

"Are you kidding me?" She shook her head. "Dino Brancuzzi would have found me by now if he actually looked. Dino Brancuzzi could find an ice cube at the bottom of an avalanche. He just never bothered."

Silence shimmered across the connection for three long beats.

"Okay, I'll give you that. But you didn't—"

"Forget about what I did or didn't do," she interrupted. "I know if I'd told him I was pregnant, everything would have been different, but I didn't want to be an obligation to him."

"I think we're past that stage now. His number one goal is to find you and keep you safe until the Blackwater crew and I take care of the bad guys."

If Dino's not going after those men himself, it means he's focused on me. But for what reason? Our relationship was so complex. Is it possible there's something there after all?

She didn't know, and she wasn't taking anything for granted. "When you talk to him, please tell him I am tucked away where no one will even think to look for me. That I'm good here until this is resolved. No lie. And I'm hanging up now."

She disconnected before he could say anything. She didn't think he could trace her location, as short as the call was. Besides, she didn't think technology was that sophisticated on Hermosa. Just to be safe, however, she'd keep this one turned off and use one of the other phones she'd bought.

The ride back to Lexie's apartment took less than fifteen minutes, although Jen had an idea that was about the average drive time to go anywhere on this island. She made a conscious effort to relax, not so easy to do. She kept wondering how long it would take whoever was behind this to find her. He might already have figured she was a red herring that Craig threw in his path, but he was also a man who hedged his bets. And just in case she even knew where those artifacts were, he'd send someone to sniff her out.

Assuming, of course, this little island even landed on anyone's radar. It was barely on the map. Most people probably didn't even know it existed.

But Dino could find it.

The thought popped unbidden into her head. Dino Brancuzzi could find anyone anywhere. How long before Hermosa was on his radar, and what would she do if and when it was?

Deanne was safe, though, and that was the most important thing.

When this was over, she knew there'd be hell to pay as far as Dino was concerned. She was sure he was mad as hell that she'd kept the fact of his daughter from him for ten years. And where did they go after this? That was the bigger question. What a mess.

****

Dino maneuvered carefully into the dock at Las Palmas. He'd called ahead to be sure he had a spot, even though he might be leaving right away. After studying the map on his tablet, he'd left Key West, urgency, frustration, irritation, and fear for Jen's safety a swirling cocktail in his gut.

He'd made short stops at the first two places, hoping to find something but not expecting to. Neither of them offered anything but frustration, which he'd known ahead of time. They were actually too small for someone to hide away on with any success, but he had to eliminate them. The islands were small enough that if by chance Jen was there, he could have pried the information loose from someone. But damn it, no one had even hinted she might be there, and he'd have known if they did.

As he berthed the boat and got ready to walk down the pier so much went through his mind.

Jen, Jen, Jen. Where are you? How can I keep you safe if I don't know where you are?

He wanted to take her and Deanne, wrap them in cotton, and really hide them away.

A daughter! He had a daughter!

God! It still seemed so unreal. Him, Dino Brancuzzi. The horn dog adventurer of all time with a child. The life he lived was in his blood, so entrenched he'd never even considered settling down. Still, there were moments when he'd been with Jen that something inside him said, "Grab this and keep it." But as quick as it came, that fast he'd dismissed it.

He'd missed Jen like hell when she disappeared, hardly daring to admit it to himself. He'd thrown himself into one thing after another, filling the space between black work cases with fishing charters. If he was busy every minute, then he didn't have time to think about how he might have screwed up.

Only now, it seemed, it was all coming home to roost and not in a pleasant way. But in that short visit, the little girl who was his daughter had made a place for herself in his heart. No matter what he had to do to accomplish it, he was going to find Jen, take care of the assholes who put her in this situation, and then beg her to marry him and make a family with the three of them.

Marry! Who'd have thought it?

Well, it wasn't going to happen if he didn't get his fucking ass in gear and find where Jen was hiding. And then keep her safe. He hoped to hell his damn luck would change soon.

He chatted with the Las Palmas customs people and the harbormaster, hung out in the marina office having a cold drink with one of the men he knew, then climbed back onto his boat. So far, today had been a big nothing. Worse than a nothing. He couldn't say he'd wasted the time, because at least he eliminated some places. But not one person he spoke to had any news of a woman like Jen showing up unexpectedly at any of the islands they were familiar with. Even some of the unfamiliar ones.

One of the questions at the top of his list was how she'd gotten out of the states. It was possible she knew someone who could create fake documents for her, but he'd checked all his sources, of which there were many, and nothing had shown up. Same thing with flight reservations. And again, if she flew under a different name, she'd have needed acceptable documentation. And also to enter any of these tiny island countries with proper documentation.

He'd made a list of the possible/probable islands where she might have found a place to hide. It would depend on who she'd been able to contact from her years on St. Thomas—if anyone—and who she might actually have connected with that might help her. But he had charted a course so he hit them in some kind of sensible order. He was still convinced that she was tucked away in a corner of the Caribbean.

An ugly thought struck him.

What if whoever was running this shit show had already found Jen? What if Sutherland had found her? Who the hell had the missing pieces right now?

No, no, he was letting his so-called mind run away

from him. Ethan was in Michigan following all those leads. Ethan was the best at this. He'd find out what was going on, who the hell the mystery buyer was, where Sutherland was, and who really had the antiquities. And the Blackwater crew was scouring its connections to see if anyone was looking for buyers for the stolen artifacts.

He decided this would be a good time to check in with Ethan. Sitting at the bar in the cabin, he punched a number in the cell phone.

"What's going on in Michigan?" he asked when Ethan answered.

Ethan barked a laugh. "Ten kinds of shit. It's a mess here, Dino. A big fucking mess."

"But we knew that."

"We did," Ethan agreed. "Anyway, it seems all hell has broken loose here. It's all over the news, television, and online. You can't get away from it. It seems the missing shipment contained some exceptional rare antiquities that the museum board was counting for a special exhibition they've been promoting. There are some really pissed off people here. With Sutherland missing, rumors are running wild that he's involved, of course. Gossip is that he's selling the missing pieces to pay his gambling debts. Debts, by the way, that the board knew nothing about and is beyond pissed off to find out."

"So it's safe to say no board members played in these high-stakes poker games?"

"You got it."

"We'd already heard most of that from Jen," Ethan pointed out. "The FBI's still here, and all the museum staff are being investigated. Now that the exorbitant value of the missing stuff has been calculated, not to mention the historical value, the crisis is even greater. And the collectors who shipped the legitimate items are planning to sue the museum, which could easily put it out of business."

"Not unexpected," Dino told him.

"They've also got people searching everywhere for Craig Sutherland. He seems to have vaporized, but we knew that. The major donors are screaming for someone's head, and they don't care whose."

"No less than I figured. Were you able to get a list of Sutherland's friends?"

Ethan snorted. "Depends on who you ask. He doesn't have a lot of people telling me how wonderful he is, though. I talked to his wife. That was a trip. She's gone completely off the rails. She said she knew nothing about this, and I believe her. I don't think she's that good an actress, but you never know. And while they live in a nice enough home, he wasn't spending his winnings on it. She was packing to leave and wanted nothing to do with me."

"Damn."

"But," Ethan continued, "I just finished talking to a guy I know."

Dino wanted to laugh. Ethan "knew a guy" in almost every corner of the earth. "I'll bet you did."

"He gave me the names of people Sutherland hung out with. I'm not talking about the ones he and his wife were friends with. I mean the ones he spent time with when he wasn't running the museum or being a poor excuse for a husband. Very much under the table. Oh, he puts on a good front. He's Mister Three Piece Suit with an advanced college degree when he's playing the part of museum director."

"And how is that working out?"

"Like he's two people. My friend says in "certain circles" it's well known that Sutherland has a bad gambling habit. Before Welborn brought him into his game, Sutherland had managed to get himself invited into the private rooms at a couple of casinos. Apparently, he loses enough to gain him entry. The question is, how was he covering his losses? He wasn't winning enough for that. Bad for his position if word got out that the director of the museum gambled and poorly. And that he didn't want to feed it in the regular casinos."

"Which of course is why he's got his side business going." Dino leaned back in his seat and stretched out his legs. "Anyone know how long he had an arrangement with Welborn? And was he doing this with anyone else?"

"I'm hoping to find out tonight." Ethan chuckled. "Okay, you called at the right time. I just got off the phone with Nick who gave me some information Guardian dug up that will help with that."

"And?"

"I don't know how they did it, but they got a list of the people who play in that very private high-stakes poker game."

A little thrill raced down Dino's spine. "Interesting people, I bet."

"You have no idea." Ethan cleared his throat. "This is a heavy list, Dino. We know Welborn was the driving force behind this. It also includes John Campbell, a hedge fund manager whose clients include the crème of the Detroit financial world. Colin Garvey, the senior partner in the biggest corporate law firm in the area. Monica McCall, wife of the lieutenant governor and herself a powerful CEO of Advantage Techtronics. Also the woman with the money and power behind her husband's political aspirations. Congressman Nathan Dekalb, whose family owns half of Detroit and the outlying suburbs."

Dino blew out a breath. "Well, fucking damn shit."

"Amen to that. And while the game is supposed to be a deep dark secret, I hear whisperings that Welborn lets it slip for his own reasons, whatever the hell they are."

"So tell me." Dino shifted in his seat. "Whether that's true or not, if this is an ultra-secret game and you have to be invited, how did Welborn decide who to invite? And why? And how did Sutherland get on the list? How did all that come about?"

"Each of these people is someone who can be useful to Welborn in his international operations," Ethan pointed out.

"Sounds like a group of people who could all help each other."

"That's probably where the idea started," Dino agreed.

"This is Welborn's playtime all the way," Ethan pointed out. "Apparently it's been happening for years. Sutherland probably wet his pants when Welborn invited him, not realizing he was being set up for something he could never get out of."

"No shit."

"Another thing," Ethan told him. "I also sniffed out that Welborn has a very private collection of art and artifacts that only he and one or two others get to see.

All forbidden or stolen items. If so, I can see why he'd be pissed if someone aced him out of these latest artifacts."

"That's the damn truth," Dino agreed.

"And Welborn is certainly in a position to manipulate the situation. He's museum chair and Sutherland's boss. He probably flattered the man by inviting him into the game, and once the noose was set, he could slowly tighten it."

"Didn't people think he was kind of the odd man out?" Dino shook his head.

"Not if others were using him for the same thing," Ethan pointed out. "Maybe he was smuggling items in for others in the group. Maybe his gambling addiction gave them the hold to pressure him to do this. I've dealt with scum like that far too often."

"Well, shit. Are you saying that's what he did?"

"Not at all. Just offering a possibility. Apparently, he's had a gambling habit for a very long time which made him vulnerable. I'm sure he was excited to be playing with people way out of his class. He'd gamble more than he should, lose his ass. Then someone could come to him with a proposition. Either he couldn't turn down the money or they threatened him or both. If that's what happened and the others are involved. Otherwise, it was a straight one on one with Welborn."

"Yeah." Dino nodded, even though he knew the friend couldn't see him. "Do this little favor for one of your friends at the card game, and I'll cut your losses. Or you'll get paid enough to cover those losses. And it just grew from there. But so far that's all it is. Rumor. We have to pin it down."

"We do. I have a source I'm hoping to meet with

who can actually do that for me."

"And by the way, Welborn might be richer than god, but he apparently isn't well liked. So why would these people want to play cards with him? We're missing something."

"I agree." Dino paused to organize his thoughts. "Okay. More important, what's the gossip about Jen?"

"Welborn jumped on Sutherland's lies and is spreading it everywhere. Some people are shocked that she would do such a thing. Others say they knew it all along. I'd say mostly people would rather blame her than Sutherland, even though he's the one with the ability to do this, not her. He's more well known. She's just a museum employee without a real support system"

"So she didn't make a lot of friends?" That didn't sound like Jen. He remembered her as a very outgoing person. Of course, having a child changes a lot of things.

A child!

Every time he thought of it anger, resentment, and need curled up in a ball in his chest. Van Dine had better come through with information for him. Then, as soon as this was wrapped up, he and Jen were going to have a Come-to-Jesus meeting.

"Not that I can find," Ethan told him. "Parents of kids Deanne played with. One of the secretaries at the museum, who's telling everyone loud and clear that Jen didn't do this. The one thing everyone who knew her says is, she's a great mother."

"I'm not surprised." Dino didn't know whether to be proud of the fact or pissed off that he'd missed so much of the chance to be a father. But once this was over that was going to change.

"How's the sunshine trip going?" Ethan asked.

Dino's laugh was anything but humorous.

"How many ways can you spell boring? I hope this doesn't turn out to be a dead end and a big waste of time. I don't think it is, but—"

"Then that's what you focus on," Ethan told him. "I gotta go meet a guy, but let's check in tomorrow morning about nine. Sooner if any of us gets anything."

"Sounds good to me."

"Good luck in the sunshine."

"Yeah." Dino snorted. "I'm gonna need it."

He disconnected and squinted off into the distance. He figured he had three more hours of good daylight to search today. He wanted to end up at one of the little islands where he could berth the boat for a while and hang out in an area where people congregated. Island bars were always good for picking up gossip, and after all these years, he knew just how to pry it loose.

But he also wanted to know who else had been looking for Jen. He had no idea how much she'd told the people she worked with or any of the friends she'd made about her life before she got to Michigan. Had she told anyone about her days in the Caribbean? What had she told them about Deanne's father? How had she explained the absence of one?

God. He'd been such an arrogant fool, so full of himself, just now realizing the pure gold he'd had in front of him all that time. Nine years! He'd missed nine years of her life. How would he ever get it back? And how would he convince her he was genuinely sorry for letting all this time go by and for not recognizing what he really felt for her? That he wasn't really the asshole he liked everyone to think he was?

Shit! What a mess he'd created.

Well, before he could start apologizing, he had to find her and hoped he wasn't too late. He pulled up the map of the area on his phone and scanned the closest islands. Big Sea Shell looked to be the best one to target. He could get there by dinnertime and hang out in the kind of place where gossip was on the menu. He hoped to fucking hell someone there knew something.

He'd made a lot of mistakes in his life, and letting Jen disappear without trying to find her was at the top of the list. Now he was going to find her and…and…and then what? He had a daughter, for fuck's sake. Time to make some decisions in his life. Make some changes. But first he had to find Jen, get her out of the line of fire, and keep her safe. And do it fast.

Chapter Nine

It was only nine o'clock, but Jen was exhausted. Meeting the guys at The Dive Shop, taking a tour of Hermosa, and moving into Lexie's apartment had done her in. Of course, she'd had little sleep in the past three days, and her nerves were strung tighter than guy wire. She was sure every shadow concealed Sutherland or someone else after her. Loud noises made her jump, and when they stopped for a casual dinner, she made sure they got a corner table. She knew Lexie was aware of all of this but fortunately didn't say anything.

Jen kept her gun with her in her purse the entire time. She didn't know what the permit situation was on Hermana, but she wasn't about to give it up. Not when people wanted to kill her. The strain, however, of always being on the alert, always being ready to defend herself, was exhausting.

When a friend of Lexie's called with an invitation for Tequila and Tortilla Night at a local bar, Jen begged off.

"I'm wiped," she told Lexie. "I think I just want to get into bed and veg."

"You don't mind if I go hang out for a while? I hate leaving you alone."

"Are you kidding?" Jen shook her head. "After everything you've done for me today? You deserve to drink the whole bottle. In fact…" She dug into her purse and pulled out a twenty. "Here. Have a couple on me."

"Oh, honey, that's not—"

"Of course it is." She tucked the bill in Lexie's pocket. "Now go have a good time. I'm going to shower and climb into bed and hope I have nice dreams for a change."

The hot shower did her more good than she imagined it would. Then, lotioned and powdered, she slipped between the sheets of the bed in the tiny guest room and was asleep almost as soon as her head hit the pillow.

And then the damn dream popped into her head. Again.

The lamps were off, but the curtains were open, allowing the full moon to shine its light into the bedroom. Dino was back.

Every day that he was gone on whatever he was doing dragged on her. She'd told herself not to fall for him. He wasn't a forever kind of guy. But god, it was hard keeping her emotions locked up where he was concerned. He was exciting, handsome, electric to be with, and the sex far outshone anything she'd ever experienced.

But she had to keep reminding herself that he could walk at any time. That's just who he was. Enough people—especially other women—had made it a point to tell her. And now, she had a secret that she knew she couldn't share with him. She wasn't sure what his reaction would be, but she was sure it wouldn't be good. She'd have to leave soon and do it in a way that she left no trace. Dino was very good at tracking people if he wanted to. Maybe he'd just get angry with her and wipe her out of his mind.

If only she could do the same.

Lecturing herself didn't help at all. It was all she'd been able to think about all day, ever since he called her from his boat to ask if he could see her tonight. What a question. Did she need air to breathe? Of course he could see her. As much of her as he wanted. She had no willpower where this magnetic, sexy hunk of a bad boy was concerned.

When they were together, she just pushed all of it to the back of her mind.

As soon as he showed up tonight, ostensibly to take her to dinner, they'd practically ripped each other's clothes off. They hadn't even made it to her bedroom. He'd taken her right against the wall in the living room, lifting her with his big hands cradling her ass as he thrust his hot, thick swollen dick into her ready and waiting pussy.

Pussy. Why was she so uncomfortable using that word when she was all in with him filling it with his fingers, his tongue, his cock?

Pressing her against the wall, he thrust into her again and again and again, positioning her so every plunge of his dick dragged against her throbbing clit. Over and over, driving them to the brink so fast she could barely catch her breath when they both exploded with the force of a hand grenade. She wrapped her legs around his hips and clung to him for dear life as the orgasm shook their very bones. They were breathless when the last tremor subsided and she was able to slide her legs down past his hips to the floor.

They stood there for a moment, shaking from the force of the orgasm, but both knowing they wouldn't be going anywhere for dinner.

He grinned, his hands cupping her cheeks. "You'll have to feed me later...after."

"After what?"

"After I finish eating every delicious inch of your body."

He picked her up, leaving their clothes on the floor, and carried her to her bedroom where he proceeded to lick every sweet part of her, nibbling at her nipples and her clit until she thought, if he didn't fuck her again pretty soon, she was going to explode with need and hunger.

Now she lay naked beneath him in her bed, her body thrumming with desire. In the softer light, Dino's hair looked jet-black, his eyes like polished onyx. The dark scruff on his jaw made him look both sexy and dangerous. The feel of his hard, firm, naked body against hers made her pulse jump and the very core of her throb with need. His calloused hands cupped her face, those dark eyes looking at her with heat blazing in them. Against her thigh, she felt the hard length of his delicious cock.

God, how she missed him when he was gone. She had no idea where he kept disappearing to. He always brushed it off by telling her a client had chartered him. But what client? Chartered him for what? What was so mysterious? It had to be dangerous, as secretive as he was about it. But then he wore danger like a cloud wrapped around him.

Stop it, she told herself. Enjoy him while he's here. God knows it was the best sex of her life, ever. He was a completely unselfish lover, creating a craving inside her that seemed to grow stronger each time they were together.

"I can't say this any plainer, Jen." His deep voice had that familiar rasp. "I couldn't wait to get back this time. I couldn't stop thinking about your naked body, every delicious inch of it. I want to fuck you. Every way possible. I want to suck your nipples and your clit. Lap the sweetness of that pretty pink pussy. Feel my dick inside you everywhere I can."

Excitement shot through her, making the walls of her sex thrum with need. Oh, god, yes. She wanted him inside her filling her, stretching her walls, igniting every tiny nerve ending.

"Yes," she said, her voice thick with need. "Do it. Fuck me. Fuck me every way you can."

"Count on it. But first, I'm going to fuck your mouth with my tongue."

He licked the outer edge of her lips, swept his tongue over their surface before thrusting it into her mouth. It was hot and wet on her tongue, setting off every nerve in her body. She wound her fingers in his thick hair, holding his head in place as she met his tongue with her own. Every inch he touched ignited nerves and sent hot signals to the rest of her body.

Finally easing his mouth from hers, he trailed his lips along the line of her jaw and down her neck, taking little nips at her skin as he did so. Soothing the tiny bites, he covered the hollow of her throat and sucked hard on it. The sensation sent electric shivers straight to the heart of her sex. She clenched her inner muscles as they flexed with need.

He took a long time kissing his way down to her breasts, teasing her, tasting her, and drawing the outline of each mound with the tip of his tongue. Shivers raced over her, spiked with desire. When he finally took one hardened nipple in his mouth and closed his teeth over it, her body tightened in response. God! She wanted his cock inside her so badly.

The man was driving her out of her mind, just the way he always did.

"Fuck me." She whispered the words, begging. "Please. Fuck me."

His laughter vibrated against her breast. "I am. I'm just taking my time at it. Can't rush a good thing. I want to enjoy every minute of this."

She had no idea how long he spent, because time stretched into one long hot spear of lust. He moved his mouth from one nipple to the other, laving them both with his tongue, scraping them with his teeth then licking them again. Every touch sent an arrow of heat straight to her core. Her sex. Her pussy. Why did she have such trouble with that word when "fuck" rolled off her tongue like melted butter?

"I want your cock inside me," she groaned. Her inner walls hungered for the feel of his thick shaft filling her.

His laughter made that very part of his body vibrate against her, raising the level of heat swamping her and ramping up her desire.

"All in good time. I want to enjoy every second."

Yes, rush it, she wanted to scream. And then do it all over again.

Her breasts ached with need by the time he finally slid his mouth down the valley between them, then lower to suck on her navel.

"You're driving me crazy," she moaned.

"Good." That sexy laugh rumbled again. "Then I'm

doing my job."

He teased the crease where her thighs and hips joined, trailing the tip of his tongue over the delicate area over and over. She moaned again and tried to push his head lower, but again that sexy laugh vibrated against her. He lifted his head and looked up at her, his eyes hot with lust.

"All in good time, hotshot. I don't want to get to the finish line before we're ready."

"I'm ready! I'm ready! Oh, god, Dino, I am more than ready."

He laughed again. Then he trailed his tongue down over her mound to the hot cleft of her sex. Her muscles clenched, wanting something to fill that space. Wanting his thick cock in there, fucking the life out of her. But instead, he continued to tease and torment until she thought she'd go insane with need. Sliding his hand beneath her ass, he lifted her to his mouth and proceeded to lick and nip every inch of the sensitive flesh.

"Please," she begged.

In answer, he slid one large finger inside her. She was so aroused that mere movement triggered an orgasm. She clenched down on him, bending her legs at the knee, digging her heels into the mattress, and riding his hand until the orgasm burst through her.

It was over way too soon, leaving her breathless and still unfulfilled. She pushed herself onto his finger, trying to coax him to using it again, but instead he slid it out, looked up at her, and carefully licked every inch of it with his tongue.

"You're driving me crazy." She gasped the words.

"Good." He grinned. "That's my plan."

He inched his big body lower so he could nudge her thighs wide apart with his shoulders. He opened the lips of her sex and took a long slow lick. Hot shivers raced over her skin at the first touch of his strong tongue. Another stroke and another. Then he took her clit between his teeth and tugged on it, gently but enough to set off a riot of sensations in every nerve ending.

"Oh, god!"

He hummed his satisfaction at her reaction, the sound vibrating through every inch of her pussy. And when he slid one finger inside her and then another it set off a cascade of vibrations that almost, but not quite, brought her to another orgasm again. He worked those fingers slowly in and out of her, but just as she nearly reached the point of release, he slipped them out and eased them down between the cheeks of her ass.

At once every one of her muscles clenched in response, and she tried to push herself into his touch. Just as she thought she couldn't stand any more he thrust his tongue into her hot core, and she exploded. She reveled in the hot contact, riding his tongue while his fingers did magic things to the cleft of her ass. Shivers raced the length of her spine, and her nipples ached for his mouth again.

He knew exactly how and where to touch her, what to do, how to draw the most response from her. He knew where every sensitive spot of her body was located and how to use his hands and his tongue for maximum effect.

The sensations built and built, Dino taking his time, not rushing, his tongue licking. The orgasm grabbed her, sending her inner muscles into hard tremors. She rode his hot tongue and his fingers until the last vibrations faded. But even when her muscles went lax, a hunger still consumed her.

"I want to touch you," she begged. "Please."

"If I let that happen," he told her in a thick voice, "I won't last two minutes." He nipped the inside of one thigh. "But later's another matter.

He dragged kisses up the inside of one leg and down the other before reaching for the condom he'd left on the nightstand. He rolled it on expertly. Then he spread her legs wide, bending them at the knee so she was completely open to him. Sliding one hand beneath her ass and lifting her, he used the other to guide his cock into her opening.

She felt the pressure of the head as he slowly eased into her, felt the pulsing of the vein that wrapped around his hot dick. Digging her heels into the bed, she shoved against him until every inch of him filled her.

"God, Jen," he breathed. "There's nothing as good as this. Look at me. Look at me while I fuck you."

She opened her eyes and saw the heat and hunger flashing in his, which only ramped up her own. God! He felt so good inside her. She didn't want this ever to stop.

He bent his head to lick her nipples, taking a little bite at each of them.

"Wrap your legs around me." His voice was heavy with lust. "Ride my cock, Jen. Do it."

His thick shaft filled her so completely that it dragged against her sensitive flesh as he moved in and out, slowly at first then faster and faster. Wrapping her legs around him, she locked them at the ankles. Her heels digging into the small of his back. They moved together in a dance so familiar to her she knew every nuance. There was nothing except the two of them and the heated movements that drove her to ecstasy every time.

And then she stopped thinking and was lost in the pleasure of it all, in the feel of him inside her, at the contact of his hard, muscular body. In and out, back and forth, heat consuming her. She felt the orgasm building deep inside her, rolling up like a wave heading for shore. And then, like the explosion of a rocket, there it was, gripping them, his cock throbbing inside her, the walls of her sex spasming against his hard, thick cock so tightly.

She didn't want this ever to end, but at some point, their bodies began to relax. Jen eased her legs down and waited for the beating of her heart to slow. Her legs fell to the side, Dino propped himself on his elbows and dusted kisses over her face before capturing her mouth in one long, deep connection. He sucked hard on her tongue then let his slide over it with a slow, delicious sweep before breaking the connection.

Easing himself from her body, he went to dispose of the condom before sliding back into bed with her.

"I'm back for ten days," he told her in his gravelly voice, pulling her against his body. "I want to spend it with you. All of it. Can you get some time off work?"

"I'll see what I can do," she promised."

But then what? Would the day come when he just left and that would be the last she'd see of him? Should she tell him…

Jen's eyes opened wide. Her mouth was dry, but her palms were sweaty, and her heart was pounding so hard she was sure she could hear it. She hadn't had erotic dreams about Dino in a very long time. She'd had to forcefully block him from her mind, or she'd have been in a bad way, longing for a man she could never have. Now she'd had two of them in a very short time, and the emotions that she felt for him threatened to swallow her whole. She needed to get this out of her head.

Except…right now, tonight, her body felt as if it had just been through a sexual marathon and her skin was covered with a fine sheen of sweat.

The one definite thing about their relationship had been the quality and intensity of their sex. Every moment with him was an explosive, erotic experience. Even now, with the dream so fresh, her body tingled from his remembered touch.

She pushed herself out of bed and made her way to the small kitchen for a glass of ice water. She needed to cool off both her body and her mind. She couldn't afford to be distracted in her current situation.

She stood at the sink drinking the water and wondering how on earth she'd managed to get herself in this mess that started out as just incredibly good times with the sexiest, most intriguing man she'd ever met. If she managed to get out of this with her skin intact, her first job would be to create a relationship between Dino and Deanne, the second would be to take a good look at the situation between her and Dino, and the third would be to take a really good look at her life and see where she could go next. Hopefully, as much as she hated to admit it, with Dino, but that was such a long shot.

What had he thought when he heard her story? How had he reacted when he met Deanne?

She tiptoed back to bed and pulled up the covers, hoping she could get enough sleep in what remained of the night to be sharp for her first day on her new job. And also to keep an eye on everything happening around her. Hermosa wasn't even on half the maps, but Dino had been doing this long enough to know you never wrote anything off and you never took chances.

Chapter Ten

Swallowing back his irritation, Roger Welborn punched a number on speed dial and waited impatiently for the call to be answered. He was getting nowhere with this situation, and he was in danger of everything he'd built falling apart. And all because some greedy little schmuck saw a chance for a big score and a chance to disappear. Even Leneghan, who had been with him a long time and knew how to clean up almost every mess, wasn't having much success. Maybe it was time to get back to his ace in the hole. A man he'd known a long time, although he scrupulously avoided having their names tied together.

To the public at large, Roger was an enormously wealthy man who headed a massive commercial conglomerate and rubbed elbows with royalty and celebrities all over the world. His wife, Melinda, was sought after for fundraisers and top-level society functions. Almost no one knew about the locked room in his house where he kept the forbidden artifacts he bought in secret. Or the bribes he paid to get his business taken care of. Or the people he'd done business with who disappeared when they became obstacles.

Peter Leneghan had been with him since he'd begun "expanding" his business and handled most of the activity he couldn't talk about. There were, however, some things even Peter would balk at, and for that he had Dante Fox. There wasn't a problem Fox couldn't handle, couldn't fix. Finding people who disappeared and extracting information from them was one of his specialties.

"It's been less than twenty-four hours," Fox said when he answered.

"I thought you were the miracle worker," Welborn growled. "That's what you always tell me, and that's what you always live up to."

Fox barked a laugh. "This miracle might take a little longer. Your girl is damn good at disappearing."

Welborn ground his teeth. "So you're telling me you haven't even got a smell of her?" That was not good at all.

"I didn't say that. I might actually have a line on her. Maybe. But the price has gone up."

"Motherfucker." Welborn spit out the word. "You holding me up?"

"No more than usual. But I had to grease a lot of palms to get even a sniff of this. Plus, it will take some extra legwork on my part."

Welborn frowned. "What the hell? Who is she that she could do such a disappearing act?"

"One smart little bitch. I have a couple of places to check, and I'm pretty sure she's at one of them."

"Pretty sure? You'd better be damn sure. How long until you check it out?"

"I have three islands in all to check, and I'm doing it myself, which is another reason for the increased cost. I don't want to send someone in who can scare her off and send her to ground someplace else." He paused. "And there's one other thing."

Welborn felt his gut tighten. "Now what?"

"There's someone else looking for her. A man named Dino Brancuzzi."

"So?"

"You don't know who he is, do you?" There was a funny tone to Dante's voice.

"No. Who the hell is he that I should even have heard of him?"

"You and he wouldn't move in the same circles, but he's known as the king of black ops, both government and as a private contractor. His nickname is Mister Invisible, because they never see him coming until the damage is done. Word is he knows twenty different ways to kill someone and even more to torture them. And he has a large undercover network."

The muscles in Welborn's gut tightened. Fuck. Just what he needed.

"Why haven't I heard of him? He can't be that important."

Fox's laugh had an unpleasant sound. "The fact that you haven't heard of him makes him even more dangerous, because there's hardly a killer not on your list. Trust me when I tell you, this is a most dangerous man. And his best friend, although he's been out of the business a while, is even more deadly. And you may have heard of this one. Ethan Caine."

"Son of a motherfucking bitch."

What the hell had he gotten himself into? All he'd wanted was the secret pleasure of owning things no one else ever could. Things he could quietly brag about to his inner circle, men with whom he'd built his business, because they, too, didn't believe in rules. When he'd discovered Sutherland's dirty little gambling secret, he thought he had a sure way to get the man under his control and force him to smuggle in pieces for his collection. The invite to the card game had stoked the weasel's ego, and after that, things fell right into place.

But what the fuck had triggered this fiasco? The saliva in Welborn's mouth dried up, and he felt the beginning of a headache. Fox was right. He did know of Ethan Caine. The man had ruined more than one situation he was aware of, fortunately not for him but for people he did business with.

Caine had worked for the government doing black ops, but he was also the man who handled dark things for Guardian Security. Caine was cold as ice and had no sympathy for anyone. Cross him and you were dead. Welborn had lost two business associates, because they thought they could outsmart the man.

"I thought he'd eased off," he said at last.

"He has. He's married and has a son, so he's cut back on the black ops, but he's not totally retired. Runs a training school out at a big farm he owns. But he and Brancuzzi are joined at the hip buddies. Together, they are a deadly duo. Good thing you tapped me, because not too many people can take on these two. Keep in mind, they have almost as many connections as I do. They could locate both the artifacts and the female before I do."

Double fuck.

Welborn sat there, everything running around in his head.

"Whatever it takes," he said at last. "I want this female and the antiquities she's hiding away. If she doesn't have them, she's got to know where they are. Either way, she's the key. Find her. Now. Whatever it takes."

"And if she doesn't have them? If it's not her but Sutherland double crossing you?"

"Then get rid of her, find him, and get it out of him," Welborn growled. "I don't care how. Use your special skills. And fucking get it done or I'm ruined."

"I thought Leneghan was on that."

"He's getting nowhere so far, and this has turned more complicated than I expected, and he doesn't have the contacts or outreach that you do. Sutherland thinks he's so fucking smart, but he's not. Unless he had his escape plan solidly in place, I know he's left a trail of breadcrumbs. Peter is following them, but…"

Fox's laugh was anything but humorless. "But you need my 'special talents' to make this work. Am I right?"

Welborn wanted to smash something, because Fox's words were so true. Losing the items he salivated over wasn't nearly as bad as having a fool like Sutherland completely fool him. If he could, he'd shoot the man himself.

"Just find that bitch," he said at last. "Soften her up and then bring her to me. And dig deep on Sutherland. I'll find out where the damn stuff is, or someone will pay a big price." A thought struck him. "Call Hammer. Have him work with you."

"Damn, Welborn. Are you sure?"

"Damn sure." Hammer could wring information from anyone.

"Whatever you want."

"That's exactly what I want. You understand that, right?" When there was no response he repeated, "Right?"

But then he realized Fox had already hung up.

Motherfucker.

He had the uneasy feeling that his life was about to undergo some changes that he wanted to avoid.

****

Dino hit one more island before he decided to drop anchor for the night at St. Amelia. He'd been there numerous times, sometimes with a fishing charter, sometimes on a black ops assignment to pick up or deliver a person who was better off nameless. The problem with St. Amelia was, word had spread that the island had become a hot spot for…pickup and delivery. It was small enough that situations could be controlled but large enough that people could melt into the environment, at least for a short while.

But there was always gossip, if you knew where to listen, and that gossip was what he was after.

He'd called ahead, as usual, to make sure there was a berth available, then pulled up the usual customs paperwork on his laptop. Once the forms were completed, he sent it to the customs officer and emailed a copy to the marina office. Finally, with a berth number assigned, he'd cruised into the dock and dropped anchor for the night.

He knew the manager of the marina fairly well after multiple visits and planned to stop at the office and talk to him, get a feel for the possibility that Jen had ended up here. Or maybe someplace else that his friend might have gotten wind of. But first he wanted to check in with Ethan again. He picked up on the first ring.

"Any luck yet?" Ethan asked.

"Nada, but this is only my fourth stop, and I

haven't really searched yet. Before we go any further, how are things back at the farm? Got any reports from Guardian?"

Ethan chuckled. "Yes, and they're all good."

"And Deanne?"

Ethan's sigh carried across the connection. "You're gonna have lots of work to do there, Daddy. She's a smart kiddo. She wants answers, and she won't be put off with anything glib. If you want a real relationship with her—"

"I do," Dino interrupted. "No shortcuts. Nothing just surface. I've been regretting the last ten years ever since this all blew up."

"Well, you know Lisa and I are here if you need us."

"I do and I appreciate it. Now. How's it going with you?"

"Interesting. Hold on."

Dino heard the sound of a door closing, then his friend was back.

"Okay. Sorry. Just wanted privacy for this. Lots going on under the surface in this high society area, although nothing really surprises me."

"Let's have it."

"The guy must be some kind of asshole. What did you find out about the gambling?"

"This is kind of a complicated story, but it's really what we figured. Welborn put the game together but outside of superficial social contacts it's not like they hung out together. I emailed Nick Vanetta and asked him to do a background check on everyone again, because I promise you, there's a deep dark secret somewhere."

"I agree." Dino nodded, even though he knew no one could see him.

"I'm also having Nick run deep profiles on the entire board of directors of the museum as well. We can't afford to overlook anyone."

"Did Nick send you detailed profiles on the other names you told me about?"

"Working on it. And I'm sniffing out gossip here, too. There's a high degree of competition among those people. They all want to one up each other, which means what we suspect is perfectly logical. Maybe one of the other players got a sniff of what Welborn and Sutherland were doing and decided he wanted a piece of the pie himself. Or herself. Or the whole pie. Got to Sutherland, offered him a shitpot of cash to grab up the whole shipment this time and sell it to them instead of Welborn."

"Or figured out how to sell it to fund his new lifestyle in a different country. Hell, with that kind of money he could settle anywhere." Dino despised people like that. Their greed and selfishness always had major repercussions. This time Jen had been caught in the tidal wave. "Anything on Welborn himself yet?"

"On the surface, very cooperative. And he knows just how to play things. If he's angry, he's only going to show it when it involves injury to the museum. Guardian is digging up everything they can on him. There's something there, probably in his past. We just have to find it."

"Yeah, no kidding." This was always the worst part of any op—digging out the information to locate people. "Any word yet on Sutherland's whereabouts?"

"Angel and Octavio are checking every source

they've ever come in contact with. He can't dispose of anything with such a high value, even a little at a time, without someone talking about it. They're hitting all their contacts. Hold on a sec. I just got a text."

Dino tried to control his impatience until Ethan came back on the line.

"Okay, Octavio says he's meeting in a few with someone who might be able to give him a lead on where the asshole could have gone to ground. Everyone's looking for him and those damn missing pieces, so there's no way he won't be found. I didn't get the impression he was savvy enough to be able to hide like this with such valuable artifacts. I can tell you he won't win any popularity contests in this area."

"It's possible he doesn't even have them anymore," Dino pointed out, "but I'd say if he's already unloaded them, either you or I would have gotten word of it. So he's still looking for buyers, probably on the black market."

"Or," Ethan said, "he's turned them over to a go-between and already disappeared with the cash. Welborn has to be ten kinds of pissed at what Sutherland has done. You know he's got his own people out after both Jen and Sutherland."

"No one's more aware of that than I am," Dino told him

"I'm taking another go at Sutherland's wife in a little while," Ethan said. "Don't let my wife hear you say this, but women can be damn sneaky."

When he found Jen—when, not if—he was going to make sure shit like this never happened again.

"Let me know if you need extra help down there," Ethan continued. "We can always tap Guardian for that."

"I guarantee I will ask if I need more people," Dino assured him, "but I'm trying to do this as low-key as possible, so I don't stir any waters. I'm just waiting to hear back now from the guy I reached out to."

"Okay. Anything else?"

"Not right now." Dino disconnected the call and sat back in his chair for a moment. Yeah, when this was all settled, he and Jen were going to have to lay all their cards on the table. He'd fucked things up enough already. His no-strings attitude had cost him nine years with a child he didn't even know he had and a relationship with a woman who he'd finally figured out was everything he'd ever wanted. What a dumb schmuck he was.

No more, though. He'd fix that as soon as he cleaned up this mess.

But first things first. There were so many loose pieces in this thing. He was convinced Sutherland gave those missing pieces to someone from the gambling circle, someone who offered him a shit ton of money to do it. And then he split, because otherwise he knew he'd be dead.

Dino locked down the boat and headed to the marina office at the end of the dock. He needed to chat with Danny Almonte, who had his fingers on the pulse of everything that happened on St. Amelia and often on other small islands. He probably should have hit him up first, but he had to eliminate the others before he could move forward.

Almonte was sitting in the chair behind his desk when Dino tapped on the door of the shack. He disconnected the phone call he was on and waved Dino inside.

"Nice to see you when it's not the middle of the night." He grinned. "Does that mean you're here for pleasure?"

"Maybe one of these days. I'm actually chasing a missing person and figured if there was any gossip about her around here, you'd know it."

Danny reached into a desk drawer and brought out a bottle of Jack Daniel's and two glasses. "I always think better with a drink in my hand." When the rocks glasses were filled Danny lifted his, clinked it against Dino's and took a swallow. "To success."

Dino nodded. "I'll drink to that."

"Okay, let's have it. Who are you hunting now?"

Chapter Eleven

Jen took a tiny sip of her fruit flavored drink, being careful to push the paper umbrella aside so she didn't poke herself in the eye. She looked around Shenanigans, a typical beach bar that could fit anywhere in the universe. Wood flooring. Appropriate items on the walls like surfboards, crossed oars, and life preservers. It might be a weekday night, but the place was still more than three quarters full with an eclectic mix of people—vacationers, SCUBA divers, sport fisherman, sailing addicts. And residents who made it all happen for them, out for a relaxed evening.

Three women Lexie was friendly with had met her and Jen there earlier but only stayed a couple of hours. They were nice, though, and didn't ask her any questions. She was a friend of Lexie's, and that was that. How did you find people like this? But they were gone now, and it was just the two of them. They'd given up their table to a party of four and taken two stools at the bar.

She had to agree with Lexie. This was definitely a no stress environment. She wondered if the people hunting her would bypass Hermosa altogether because it was so low-key. Then maybe she could just stay here forever, make a new life for herself and Deanne.

Right. Fat chance.

Of course, on the other hand, they might think this

was just the kind of place she'd pick to hide. God. She had to stop driving herself crazier than she was. If she ever got out of this mess, she still had her daughter's future to worry about, especially now that Dino was aware of her existence. Dino! Another obstacle to her hiding away. She hadn't been able to scrub him from her mind after last night's hot erotic dream. Even now her body still had residual tingles. It all left her so conflicted about the entire situation. For the first time in a long time, she had real regrets about running off the way she had.

Can't go back. Can not go back.

But maybe, if he forgave her, they could go forward. For Deanne's sake, if nothing else.

First, they had to get past this.

She was sure he was sniffing out her trail even as she sat here. He was a man with many contacts, so she was sure, sooner or later, he'd find her. She just prayed that all this would be resolved before that happened.

At least it hadn't made the news in Hermosa, as far as she knew. She checked a news website on her phone as often as she could without someone asking her what she was looking for. Of course, from her impression of the customers at The Dive Shop today, she figured they came to this out-of-the-way island to get away from the news and everything it dragged with it.

Lexie nudged her arm. "What's going on? You look like you're a million miles away."

"Just reviewing some stuff from today." She took another sip of her drink.

"Uh huh. Because it was all so complicated, right?"

Jen forced a smile. "As a matter of fact, it was actually fun. And yes, ringing up the money from lessons and the sale of merchandise isn't exactly taxing. People apparently don't come here to be difficult."

"Same with the hotel shop. This is kind of the no frills ultimate escape."

Which was why it was such a good place for her to hide. If she was lucky, this island wasn't even on Dino's radar.

Lexie nodded. "Which is exactly why I like it. I can just be myself here, not some high-adrenaline party girl."

"It's only been one day, but I have to agree. The place is great. Thanks again for making it possible for me to come here."

"Happy to do it."

"How about another drink, ladies?" Jack, the bartender, grinned at them across the bar.

Lexie nodded. "Absolutely." She nudged her empty glass toward him.

Jen frowned at her own nearly empty glass. Should she? She didn't want to get too relaxed and blurt out something she shouldn't.

"Come on," Lexie urged. "One more won't hurt. I promise to make sure you don't misbehave."

Jen knew that misbehave was a euphemism for "saying something you shouldn't." She still couldn't get over the fact that this woman she hadn't seen in ten years had tuned into the fact she had a problem and without question was doing what she could to help. When this was all over, she'd have to do something really nice for her.

"Okay, but just one. And then I think I'll be ready to call it quits for the night."

As she sipped her drink, she let her gaze roam over

the room again. No one seemed out of place to her, but then, how would she know?

"Well, Jack, I see business is good as usual."

Jen had been facing Lexie, but at the sound of the male voice, she turned. A man had taken the suddenly empty stool next to her and was chatting with the bartender. She guessed him to be about five ten, with a thick head of dark hair threaded with silver. Dark eyebrows. High cheekbones. Eyes almost navy blue. He hadn't said or done anything to make her nervous, but there was something about him that created a sense of unease. Every muscle in her body tightened even though she tried to maintain a relaxed appearance. There was no way anyone could have tracked her here. At least not this fast. Her nerves were just working overtime.

The man smiled at her, a surprisingly friendly and relaxed curve of his lips. She nodded and turned back to Lexie. Although her pose was casual, she was tuned into his conversation with Randy.

The bartender chuckled. "Not bad for a weeknight. Right? So what brings Martin Van Dine to our sleepy, lazy little island? You taking one of your usual trips?"

Usual trips?

Don't get overexcited, Jen. He could be a perfectly legit businessman who travels between the islands.

"Just taking care of some business. No big deal. You know me."

Randy laughed. "Yes, I do. That's why I asked. Well, anyway, it's good to see you. Doing something for one of your mysterious clients?"

Despite herself, Jen felt every muscle in her body tense.

"Mysterious clients?" The man chuckled. "I think you have me confused with someone else. I'm just hanging out. Taking it easy."

"Yeah, right," Randy snorted. "So how long will you be here?"

"Only until tomorrow. I ended up close to Hermosa, so I thought I'd drop anchor and spend the night. Couldn't do it without saying hello and having a drink at Shenanigans."

"Got you covered." Randy reached behind him for a rectangular bottle filled with a dark golden liquid, dropped some ice cubes in a rocks glass, and poured a sizable drink.

"Ladies." He looked over at Jen and Lexie. "Can I buy you a drink? It would be my pleasure."

Before Jen could say anything, Lexie popped up. "Thanks, we're good."

The man picked up the glass, nodded at Randy, and took a long slow sip. "Just what I needed. Thanks."

"So what's new in your world?"

The man shrugged. "Oh, you know, a little of this, a little of that. Anything new going on here I should know about?"

Randy laughed. "Not in the last fifty years unless you count new plumbing and a better Internet setup. Gotta take care of our visitors. Hotel's had a little facelift. Oh, and I heard that piece of land on the other side of the island is about to be sold. Gossip says it'll be another guest facility, only this one is all bungalows."

"I'll have to take a look. Well, see you tomorrow."

"Be sure to stop by again before you leave."

"Will do." He tossed back the rest of his drink, dropped some cash on the bar, and pushed off his stool.

"See you tomorrow" He nodded at Jen and Lexie. "Ladies. Enjoy your evening."

Jen managed a smile, but there was something about the man that sent a little chill down her spine. About his whole conversation with Randy. She couldn't have said what. He certainly didn't look threatening, but her nerves sent up a warning flare as she watched him casually survey the bar on his way out. Had someone hired him to find her? Or maybe he was looking for Sutherland. But why on this tiny island that hardly anyone had ever heard of?

Or maybe that was the reason. Because she wasn't the only one who found out about Hermosa and decided it was enough off the beaten path to hide out. Had he heard something that brought him here? Because no way did she believe he was just someone who hung out in different places.

"Friend of yours?" she asked Randy?

"Martin? I don't think he's anyone's friend, really. He's just everyone's acquaintance if you know what I mean."

"Oh. Where does he live? What does he do?"

Lexie laughed. "Jen, why are you giving him the third degree about some stranger? A guy who was here for maybe two minutes."

Because sometimes they were the ones you had to watch out for.

She shrugged. "Just curious. Maybe he's here to do some scuba-diving."

"You've worked there one day and already you're looking for clients?" Lexie grinned. "Those guys must have really treated you good."

She shrugged. "It was fun."

And she might need to be afraid of that, because what if someone had set him to finding her while he did "a little of this and a little of that."

No. She was going to put it out of her mind. But she was going to find a way to keep track of Martin Van Dine. And also make herself as much in the background as possible.

"You know," she told Lexie, "I can't tell you why, but that man gives me a very uneasy feeling."

Lexie nodded. "Too smooth. Too casual. You and I have the sad misfortune of knowing too many people like that."

But she'd better be careful. Hermosa had seemed ideal when Lexie insisted she come down here. Maybe, in twenty-four short hours, it had become unsafe. She needed to figure out what to do and quickly.

****

Dino had just poured a fresh cup of coffee when his cell rang. He looked at the display. Ethan.

"I hope you're calling for more than to just say hello," he told his friend.

"Can I take a minute to complain that I'm freezing my balls up here in the northern tundra?" he joked.

"Okay. A minute. Let's have it."

"Just met with a guy who thinks a Detroit Lions sweatshirt is the height of fashion but who gave me the lowdown on Welborn and Sutherland. His name's Joe Pizzaro."

"He's plugged in?" Dino asked. They needed solid, verified information and he didn't know Joe Pizzaro from fuck all.

"One hundred percent," Ethan assured him. "Not to mention he had me checked out down to my shoe size before he'd meet with me."

"So give already. Jen's out there god knows where in danger she can't even see and time is valuable."

"He has all the gossip about Jen, Welborn. Sutherland and the missing pieces. Said the Fed are all over everything like flypaper. Word on the street now is Sutherland had a little side hustle going. Seems he was adding a few smuggled pieces of his own to shipments to the museum and selling them to Welborn. Used the money to pay his gambling debts."

"Well, fucking shit." Dino spat the words. "That's just asking to get your head chopped off." He tightened his fist on the phone. "Did he involve Jen in this?"

"There's nothing solid to indicate it," Ethan told him. "Pizzaro believes she was just a handy scapegoat when it started to fall apart."

If Dino could get his hands around Sutherland's neck right now he'd squeeze until the man's head popped off.

"So how the fuck did it blow up?"

"Like other things," Ethan told him. "Sutherland got greedy, wanted a big payday and grabbed the whole shipment."

"Well, shit." Dino wanted to pound something. Or someone. "And left clues pointing to Jen, right?"

"You got it. Now he and the missing pieces are in the wind. Welborn's out the museum shipment plus the pieces he was buying illegally. He's got his nuts in a crank over getting the stuff swiped out from under him and he's not taking it very well."

"But at least he's still walking around and trying to resolve this. Jen's off at god knows where with half the crooked art world after her and no protection. As

Sutherland's assistant she was the easiest one for him to point to. Ethan, if we don't get this cleared up she'll be in hiding forever and her life will be in the toilet."

"I'm checking the people from the card game, too," Ethan told him. Top of the line. A lieutenant governor. One of the most powerful women in the corporate world. Others like them."

"And Sutherland didn't think it was odd when he got an invite to join a group way out of his social and business circles?"

"I think his ego was so stroked he didn't ask questions," Ethan told him.

"I believe it."

"Dino, this is a lot bigger than some penny ante snuggling operation. I'm gonna widen the net. Make it really big."

"Do it," Dino told him.

"If in fact she's still alive," Ethan reminded him.

Anger surged through him, topped with a heavy layer of fear for Jen.

"I'm waiting right now for a callback from my friend who has his fingers in every pie in the Caribbean," he reminded Ethan.

"I hope to fucking hell he has news and I can get Jen to safety," Dino snapped.

"No shit. But we'll get it done," Ethan assured him. "We always do."

Dino hoped to hell he was right.

Chapter Twelve

Roger Welborn was in his den, seated at his desk, the large screen television turned to the news, which today featured the damn story about the missing antiquities. It had only been on the local stations until today, but with the FBI getting no results so far, it had gone national. He had the sound muted. It was bad enough watching the crawl across the bottom of the screen. He didn't have to listen to the fucking reporter, too.

He'd expected it being the kind of story that it was. Still, he was sure all it would do was drive Sutherland and whoever had the antiquities deeper underground. All it did was frustrate and anger him. He really should turn it off. When he finally found out who had those items, he might kill them with his bare hands.

He was still cursing under his breath when his cell phone rang. He looked at the readout on the screen.

Hammer.

He knew the definition of that word—attack or forcefully brutalize, the code name chosen by the man calling him and very appropriate. Hammer was his go-to person for dirty deeds, the ones Peter preferred not to know about, just as Dante Fox was. He'd set Hammer to searching out Sutherland when Leneghan had so far failed to find him. His warped sense of humor in the code name he'd chosen irritated Welborn, but he tried to ignore it. Because that was how the man got answers to complete his assignments.

He answered on the second ring.

"Fox contacted you," he said by way of greeting.

"He did."

"If you've got results for me already, I'll add a bonus."

"I always get results." The man on the other end of the call spoke in a harsh, gravelly voice, the result of an age-old injury to his larynx. An incident that created the man he was today.

"And?" Welborn was in no mood for word games. "Tell me, and when it's verified, I'll send your fee in the usual manner."

In the complex society the world had turned into, he now paid debts like these in bitcoin.

"He's on the woman's trail, and I've got the man. He changed his name and is living on a fancy—but not too fancy—boat in a marina in Baja California. We just have to narrow it down to which marina." His laugh sounded like sandpaper. "Makes him more mobile than living on land."

"He can't run far enough to get away from me," Welborn growled.

"Figured."

"And I suppose you just happen to have a friend in Baja? Because I don't have actual proof that he stole these things." Welborn ground his teeth. "If there was any, the Feds would have arrested him right away. He did a good job throwing shade on the woman. What about the missing pieces? I need proof that he's the one who took them."

"No problem," Hammer assured him. "Apparently,

he still has some of them, because the word is out that he's looking for buyers. Although—and don't blow a gasket—my sources tell me he's already managed to sell a couple of them. He's having trouble unloading the rest exactly because the word is out, and not just from you, the FBI, and others. I hear the donor who shipped them to the museum for a showing is ready to cut off his head. Sutherland flew to the Baja California, bought a boat, and found a place to live on it while he tries to unload the artifacts he stole."

Welborn let it all run through his mind. "And the woman?"

"No sales activity there, but she could just be waiting for the shit to die down.

"I want them both." He thought for a moment. "I'll send our mutual friend after Sutherland. You find and grab the woman. If I have them both in the same place at the same time, I'll get the truth out of them about whose idea this was. Damn it, I have to find out why he double crossed me after all this time. I'm looking forward to providing him with some unpleasant moments. I'd be happy to torture the little shit myself. I want to send a message not to fuck with Roger Welborn."

"I'm on it. What about Leneghan?"

"I'm going to have him concentrating on locating the pieces already sold and getting them back, however he has to."

"On it. And don't forget the bitcoin payment for the work so far."

"Do I ever?"

The line went dead. Not unusual. Hammer wasn't much for greetings and goodbyes. He resisted the urge to throw the phone across the room and instead punched in Peter's number into his cell.

"I have a couple of little trips for you to take," he said when the phone was answered. "I hope you like warm weather."

When he finished, he disconnected the call. He looked forward to torturing the information out of that asshole Sutherland and the woman, too. He had to send a clear message. He wouldn't rest until he destroyed everyone and got what he believed was rightfully his.

****

The phone rang, and Dino snatched it up when he saw Angel's name on the readout.

"Yeah?"

"Anything new?"

"I wish. All I get from everyone is Sutherland was a smarmy weasel, but no one seems to know where he disappeared to."

"How the fuck did an idiot like him go to ground like this?" Dino wanted to know.

"Can't answer that. Everyone's asking questions, from the FBI to the local cops to some very unsavory people." He paused. "Any word on Jen yet?"

"No, damn it." Dino wanted to put his fist through something. The more time passed, the more worried he became and the more urgent the situation grew.

Please, if there is a god, let me find her before someone else does so I can start over and build a life with her. And Deanne.

"We also learned," Angel added, "that someone is reaching deep into the black market on the dark web. Promoting some very special items for the right price."

"That's gotta be Sutherland," Dino told him.

"Uh huh. It teases about some very rare items for sale. But we need a place on the dark web."

Dino ran names through his brain. "Give me a couple of minutes. I think I still have someone who can create one."

"Okay, but you need to do it soon."

"Understood. Back to you shortly."

He disconnected the call and dialed a number he hadn't used for a very long time. For all he knew it was a dead end and the person had long since moved on. He was actually shocked when the person on the other end answered.

"Are you dead and calling me from hell?" a gravelly voice asked.

Dino barked a short laugh. "Anything is possible."

"Since only two people have this number," the voice went on, "and we haven't connected since the ice age, I'm going to assume you need a favor."

"I always said you were sharp." Dino quickly outlined what he needed. "Can you do it, and make it happen within the next fifteen minutes?"

"Jesus. Same old Dino. Yes. I'll call this number back as soon as it's done."

The line went dead, but Dino didn't worry. The man said yes, so he was on top of it.

It was almost fifteen minutes to the second when the man called back and recited an email address.

"Delete it when you're finished with whatever you're using it for."

"No problem and thanks. I owe you."

"Yes, you do," the man agreed and hung up.

Dino texted the email address to Angel with a note—*Do it now.*—

He hoped to hell this turned out to be something.

Dumping the stale coffee in his mug, he grabbed a bottle of water from the fridge, then dropped into a chair on deck. So much needed to be done, but there was also so much information he needed. Waiting was the hardest part of this process, but he didn't want to make a mistake.

Come on, everyone. Get your shit together and call me.

****

He was trying without success to force his mind to unkink, when his phone chimed. He looked at the readout. Van Dine. At least the icon he used to identify himself. Thank fuck.

"Tell me you have good news," he told the man.

"I have good news."

Dino sat up straight, a combination of tension and expectancy running through him. "You found her?"

"I did, and through a weird circumstance of events. And don't ask me about that," he added quickly. "You know my rules."

Dino snorted. "Yeah. Don't ask, don't tell, or you end up on the blacklist."

Van Dine chuckled. "Glad you still remember the rules."

"As if I'd forget. And you're sure it's Jen? No mistake?"

"The picture you sent was a few years old," he answered, "but although she's a little older, she hasn't changed much. No, it's her. You know me. But some things to keep in mind."

Dino gritted his teeth. He wanted to get going. "What?"

"I only saw her for a few minutes, but she's skittish. And she's with a friend."

What?

"Male or female?" Dino snapped.

Van Dine actually laughed. "Female. A little jealous, are we?"

Hell yes. He'd fucked up with her once. He wasn't about to do it again and let her hide out with another man.

"Just give it to me."

"I snooped around a little once I identified her. She's staying with a friend she knew from St. Thomas and she's working at the marina. At a dive shop. If she knows your boat, she'll spot it when you pull in."

"She's never seen this one," Dino assured him. "Now, where is she?"

"On a little island called Hermosa. Ever heard of it?" he asked.

God! She was that close already?

"Not until I looked on the map for little known and out of the way places," Dino told him. "How did she even find it?"

"You'll have to ask her."

"Do you know her physical location on the island?" He didn't want to have to start questioning a bunch of strangers. That would send up too many red flags.

"Not where she's spending her nights. I heard she just got there a couple of days ago, but this friend she's with got her a job with a dive shop called—don't laugh—The Dive Shop."

What the hell did Jen know about scuba-diving? Maybe she just worked in the shop itself. Anyway, that was going to come to an end before she knew it. "Martin, thanks for this."

"Good luck. Because my sources tell me Welborn's got some hotshot on her trail and probably isn't far behind you. So you'd better get her ass out of there ASAP."

"On it. And Martin? I owe you big for this one."

"Indeed you do. And you know I'll collect."

The connection went dead.

Dino realized there'd be no sleep for him tonight, so he decided to head for Hermosa. He searched it on his tablet and realized it was such a nonentity that it turned out to be a good place for Jen to hide. The problem was, if Van Dine could find her in this tiny place, whoever else was on her trail could, too. There were men like Van Dine out there who didn't care about dirty money and dirty deeds.

He also checked the details of the island's marina and realized they had a twenty-four-hour number— unusual for a place that size—where he could grab an empty berth for himself. And luckily, there was one.

He called the marina where he was now anchored and left a message that he'd received a call and had to leave. They had his credit card info so no worries there. He brewed a strong pot of coffee in the little galley, filled a tall thermos mug, and took it up to the wheelhouse. Then he went about casting off and, with his running lights on, headed out into deep water. He could have used a few hours' sleep, but he'd gone longer without it and still functioned. Of course, he'd been a little younger then, but the training never left you.

Once he was out on the open water, he took his

tablet and pulled up the information on the one marina listed. Not every small marina had guest slips to use while checking to see if one was available. Thankfully, this one did, and they were easy to pull into. Then he did a search for The Dive Shop and pinpointed its location at the marina. It was right at the entrance to one of the three docks so easy to access. The problem was keeping himself out of sight until Jen got there and he could reveal himself. He didn't know if she'd be glad to see him or yell for the cops.

Well, no. No cops. She wouldn't want to call attention to herself any more than she had to. He'd have to do this carefully, try not to scare the shit out of her, and convince her that if she wanted to stay alive, he was her best option.

But if she doesn't trust me enough to tell me about Deanne, will she trust me with her life?

He didn't remember the last time he felt this conflicted. He was still arguing with himself as he finished the second thermos of coffee and eased into the harbor of Hermosa. Two of the guest slips were empty, tiny lights outlining them for ease of access. He pulled into one and tied up the boat.

He needed someplace to take Jen after he got her into the boat, and it had to be someplace people wouldn't look for him. He certainly couldn't take her back to Key West. Surely by now, with so much at stake, people would have connected his name to hers. If they even thought he'd managed to grab her, Key West would be the first place they'd look, as well as any place close to it.

Apparently, they don't think I'm too smart. Big mistake.

That also meant staying away from people and places they might connect with him. He opened the map to study it again. He knew the Caribbean like the back of his hand. They'd figure he might head for the mainland, away from his natural territory, which was why he had to find a place there to hide away with Jen until the assholes after her were caught.

Luckily, he'd done some way off the books black work for a highly influential person who just happened to own his own island he called La Cascada, because of its outstanding waterfall. It was hardly on any map and would be an ideal place to drop anchor and keep Jen out of harm's way. He'd text Van Dine to thank him once they were well away from Hermosa.

He wished Ethan would call so he could run this by him. Finding Sutherland and the antiquities was a priority, but Jen's safety came before that. Dino knew he could never be one hundred percent sure that something was secure. In these days of the dark web and secret activities, there was always the chance of leakage. He just prayed no one would find them until Sutherland and the antiquities had been found. Welborn had to be on a rampage and his first target would be Jen.

Motherfucker.

But at least this would give them the opportunity to have a discussion about something that was at the top of his list. Deanne.

Looking at his watch, he figured he had three hours until daylight, so he settled himself in the cabin and set the alarm on his watch.

When it was fully light, Dino texted the man he was looking for, hoping the cell number still worked.

People like him usually changed phones and numbers with regularity, but he answered the text almost immediately.

—Tied up in a business meeting but will get back to you ASAP. Hope this is okay.—

Okay? He was ecstatic the man had even remembered him and answered his text. It always amazed him when clients responded this way, even though he'd usually done extreme things for them.

"You're one of a kind," a client once told him. "Honest, reliable, dependable, and you keep your mouth shut. That last especially is worth a lot."

He texted back. *—Thank you. I wouldn't bother you if this wasn't in the nature of a personal emergency.—*

—Whatever it is, I am glad I can help. Back to you as quick as I can.—

Along with the message was information on the estate, the dock, and the manager.

Chapter Thirteen

A half hour later Dino had cleaned himself up, shoved a donut in his mouth, and eased over to The Dive Shop. There was a coffee shack not far from the dive store and, while he was pretty coffeed out, he realized he could hang out at one side of it and watch for Jen without being spotted.

Two seconds later, his phone rang.

"Yes?"

"Van Dine. I've got news, and it isn't good."

Dino's stomach knotted. "Let's have it."

"Welborn apparently is connected to two men who are behind a darker curtain than I am. I know you've heard of them. Dante Fox and a man who just calls himself Hammer."

Fuck.

Yes, he knew them, and they were the worst of the worst.

"He's got them on the hunt for both Craig Sutherland and Jennifer LaCroix. With orders to get those artifacts and then kill them. Both of them. Leaving no traces. It's only been a couple of days since she disappeared, but these men can find anyone anywhere and fast."

Double fuck.

"So if you've found her, Dino, get her the hell out of there and stashed away until this matter is resolved.

Although that could be easier said than done."

Dino's hand tightened on the cell.

"What you really need," Van Dine went on, "is a place where you can make a stand and take them out. Otherwise, you'll be running forever, and I know that's not you."

"I don't like the idea of using Jen as bait."

"Jesus, Dino. Neither do I, but the fact is, she already is bait. So make it work for you. You can protect her while taking them out. But this way, you can bring them to you and get rid of them before she really gets hurt."

Dino snorted. "Why Martin, are you telling me to kill someone?"

"Did I say kill? Did I even use that word? Just find a place that is more familiar to you than them. I know you can take it from there. Meanwhile, if you've still got Caine on the artifacts, find someone else to hand that off to. Or not. Let Welborn's men grab Sutherland. Or send a different team to make sure it gets wrapped up right. Whatever happens, you can bet it will be all over the news so Jen will be off the hook but not until then. Right now her safety is your top priority."

"No shit. I should have her any minute." *I hope.*

"Then grab her and get moving. Now." He hung up without another word.

At that moment, as Dino was wondering how much worse things could get, Jen arrived. She headed for The Dive Shop, which the two guys who owned it were just opening. He took a moment to look at her as she headed to the shop. Ten years had been good to her. She was a little rounder, a little fuller, but in a very delicious way. Her hair, which she had worn shorter when he knew her, was much longer now and pulled back in a thick ponytail that bounced as she moved. He was so fascinated with the sway of her hips, he had to mentally kick himself to pay attention to business.

He didn't want to scare her, at least more than he expected to, so he followed her to the dive shop.

****

Jen was waiting for one of the two owners to unlock the dive shop when a voice behind her spoke, shocking the hell out of her. She whirled around so fast, stabbing him with her elbow, that he didn't have time to get out of the way. Instinct told her to run, but a hand closed over her arm.

"Jen. Don't scream. It's Dino." He grabbed her wrists and turned her to face him.

Dino? Dino Brancuzzi? Here, on the tiny little island? For a moment, she wondered if the dreams she'd been having, the wishes she'd made, had conjured him out of thin air. Well, she'd wanted him, and somehow, now, here he was.

"It's okay," he told her.

"Hey!" One of the guys opening the shop walked up to them. "Take your hands off her."

"Tell them it's okay," Dino said in a low voice.

She stared at him for a moment, then nodded. "It's okay, Matt. It's just someone I haven't seen in a long time. It's all good."

Matt looked from one to the other, skepticism etched on his face.

"If you say so, but we're right here. We've got your back. You holler if you need us, okay?"

"Yes." She nodded. "Thanks." Then she looked at Dino. "It's a miracle I recognized you after all this time.

What are you doing here? You scared the life out of me."

"That wasn't my intention." He cleared his throat. "Look. I know I'm the last person you were expecting. Maybe the last one you ever want to see, but Jen? It's important that I talk to you. Can we just step aside here for a minute, out of the way of foot traffic? Please?"

Instinct told her not to walk away with him, but her dreams were still active in her brain. At least she had to find out why he showed up now, after all this time. "Why are you here?"

"Not out in the open. Please, Jen."

She had so many thoughts running around in her brain, so many voices telling her not to do this, but finally she nodded. He took her hand, gently but firmly, and led her to a couple of benches on the other side of the coffee vendor. They were pretty much hidden from sight the way they were placed, but one thing she was sure of. He wouldn't hurt her.

"If you're here to yell at me about Deanne," she told him, "go ahead and get it over with."

He shook his head. "That's not why I'm here, although we're definitely going to talk about it. Right now, though, we have much more pressing business."

"Like what?" She kept her face expressionless, not wanting to give anything away. How much did he know? Was her situation the reason he was here? How the hell had he even found out about it? Oh, Ethan of course. Dummy. You knew he'd get Dino on the phone ASAP, especially after you disappeared.

"About the dangerous situation your former boss has put you in. Like that."

"Oh." She couldn't argue with him.

"Ethan gave me all the details. You did a good job disappearing, but, Jen? They have resources you can't imagine, and they already know where you are."

For a moment, she felt dizzy. Could things possibly get any worse? "But who— But how—"

"Same way I tracked you down. Listen." He rubbed his jaw. "I have no idea how you feel about me except I have to believe you know you can trust me. And I'm telling you we have to get you out of here right now. And I mean this minute."

"But—" she began again. Where could she go?

"Now, Jen," he insisted. "Or Deanne's gonna be missing a mother."

"Okay." What choice did she have? "Let me just tell the guys I have to leave suddenly. I bet they'll love that." She started to rise from the bench.

Dino grabbed her arm. "No. You can't say anything to anyone. People following the same trail I did will question them, and you can't depend on them to lie. These people have painted a target on your back."

"I at least have to call, um, the person who helped me get here."

A muscle twitched in Dino's cheek, a sign his patience was coming to an end. "Text her. Right now. And be quick about it."

While she typed in her message, he studied new boats entering the harbor. She was sure he was looking for anything that would send up a warning flag. When she was finished, he took the phone from her, pulled out the SIM card and tossed it in a trash barrel.

"That's my only phone," she protested.

"We'll get you another one when you need it,

which is not going to be in the immediate future. Forget it, forget your clothes and anything else you have here. We need to move, Jen. Now."

She knew him well enough to see he was ready to bite nails in frustration. Even as he talked to her, he continued to scan the area around them. His sole focus was undoubtedly to get her out of here. If he was that focused, things had to be worse than she thought, so why fight it? She'd left Michigan to get away from the danger. And there was no question Dino could give her the best protection.

Finally, she nodded and rose from the bench. Dino took her arm and guided her in a roundabout way to the dock where the guest slips were. They were half way down the dock when his hand tightened on her arm.

"Shit." He said the word so softly she almost didn't hear it.

"What?" She started to stop, but he kept propelling her forward.

"Just keep moving."

The only thing that she could see that might have triggered his reaction was a man walking along a parallel dock, looking casual but also taking in everything around him.

"Friend of yours?" she whispered.

"Nobody is friends with Dante Fox. He's a ton of bad news. There's no reason for him to be here except to be looking for you. Martin Van Dine was right. I guarantee you Welborn reached out to him. He can get to the same dark corners I do, which is why he's right on our tail."

An icy finger stroked her spine.

"We don't have any time to waste," he continued.

"We need to get the hell out of here right now."

Then they were at his boat, and he was pushing her up the ladder. As she stepped onto the deck, he grabbed her by the waist and led her below decks. "The minute we're away from here you're going to tell me why you're carrying."

"Stay down here out of sight," he ordered. "I'm going to cast off and start the engines. When we're out of the docking area, you can come up here."

Jen felt as if they were moving in slow motion, but finally, finally, he called down into the cabin.

"You can come up here now. We're out of the harbor and into open water. And tell me why you're wearing that gun."

She stiffened as she climbed the last step, then relaxed slightly. "Because people are after me and I need to protect myself. And don't worry. I know how to use it."

He grunted and indicated the bench along one side of the boat. "Have a seat. I reached out to a client earlier, and he texted me he's free to talk now.

He steered the boat and dialed the number on his cell.

"This is a good friend?" she asked as he waited for an answer.

She was aware that Dino Brancuzzi knew people in every corner of the earth.

"He once told me anything he could ever do for me, just call and tell him. I'm going to assume that still holds."

His conversation with his friend was brief. Although he turned away from her when he spoke, she heard enough to know what he wanted was to use the island in the Caribbean that the man owned.

"You know I don't like to ask favors," he said into the phone, "but this is a special circumstance."

Because of her? Did that mean after all these years he had special feelings for her? That she might have made a huge mistake running off the way she did? But how was she to know? He'd never given any indication that she was anything more than a good time.

He explained exactly where he was and what he needed, then waited for an answer.

"I don't even know how to thank you," Dino told the man. "I'll head there now, after I lay a little false trail down. Thanks again."

Dino disconnected the call and shoved the phone in his pocket.

"You found a place to take me." A statement, not a question.

He nodded. "Jen, you are in a dangerous situation right now. Some pretty bad people are after you and I am not going to let them get you."

"Because you feel guilty," she guessed. "For whatever reason."

"Yes, but for a very good reason." He set the wheel and motioned her over to his side. "I wasted a lot of years because I was too stupid to realize how I felt about you or how good we could be together. I'll never stop being sorry for that, but I'm definitely going to make up for it."

"For what?" She wanted him to say the specific words.

He cupped her chin. "For never telling you I love you."

He pressed his lips to hers, warm and soft, and his

scruff beard tickled her chin. His tongue traced the seam of her mouth, licking gently before exerting the slightest pressure. The taste of him was familiar even after all these years, warm and sensuous and erotic. She let herself fall into the sensuality of it, her breasts aching for his touch, her nipples suddenly hard, a pulse throbbing between her thighs.

Holy shit!

Jen allowed herself the luxury of Dino's sultry kiss, her body pressed to his as her pulse raged and her breathing quickened. God! They had come together like two hormonal teenagers, and the impact had been all-consuming. But she couldn't help but wonder if Dino kissed her out of guilt. Was he trying to lull her into a feeling of security? Erase the fact that in ten years he'd never looked for her? Or that he was feeling guilty about Deanne?

Dino finally lifted his head and brushed a kiss over her lips.

"I can hear that brain working," he teased. "Whatever's going on in there, forget it. I'm here to stay, for both you and Deanne. I missed out on too many years with both of you, and I'm not losing out again. So get that out of your head."

"Are you sure?" she asked.

Another light kiss.

"Absolutely. The two of you are what's important to me. I'm not letting either of you get away again, so understand that you're stuck with me." He swept a kiss over her lips. "This is forever, Jen. And I mean it."

For the first time since he'd grabbed her off the island, she actually believed this was happening.

"Okay." Dino shifted so he could look at Jen's

face. We have a lot to talk about. First, I made a big mistake never telling you how I felt but truth be told, emotions scared the shit out of me."

"I know that." She nodded. "That's why I never said a word. I didn't want to be an obligation to you."

"That's not gonna happen. We have a lot of time to make up for. Once this shit is taken care of we're building a life together."

A tiny thrill raced through her. She hated what had brought this about but she wasn't going to screw it up.

"Next, the gun. When did you start carrying? Before this trouble?"

Jen bit down on the instant flash of anger. This was Dino. He had no idea what she'd been doing, and it seemed his protective instincts were exploding. "I learned to shoot when I arrived in Michigan. And I'm damn good, I want you to know. The house we lived in was on the edge of town, so I bought the gun for protection. It just made sense to take it when we left with all those people after me."

She saw him struggling not to chew her out, but finally, he just shook his head. "Can't argue with that. Still, I can't say I'm excited that you find it necessary to carry a gun. And I've got a million questions, as you can imagine."

"I'm sure you do." She was sure he'd want to know everything, especially under the circumstances.

"Before we get to that, though, I want to let you know Ethan is all over this."

"I figured. When I left Deanne with him, I knew he'd start digging. Right after he called you, of course."

He nodded. "Smart move. Best move under the circumstances, because that's who he is."

Jen nodded. "I really didn't mean for him to get involved. I just couldn't think of a better place for Deanne. Although I guess in the back of my mind I hoped he'd try to help me."

"He's trying to locate those antiquities." Dino said. "He figures that will lead him to Craig Sutherland. He's got my crew helping him, plus a couple of his old contacts have come through for him. And there's something else."

"What?"

"Did you get a look at the man walking along the dock when we were leaving Hermosa?"

She nodded. "I did. Who is he? You didn't seem too happy to see him."

"I wasn't. I know who he is. One of my sources told me Roger Welborn hired him to find you. And he may not be the only one after you."

"What?" She felt the blood drain from her face. "Then...then it's a damn good thing I learned to shoot."

"Yeah, it's a bonus, but I don't plan for you to be in a position to use that gun." He grabbed one of her hands and gave it a gentle squeeze. "Jen, listen to me. I got you off that island just in time, and you're as safe as possible as long as you're with me. I plan to keep it that way." "But you will never be safe, no matter where you are, until these people are dealt with and the situation resolved. Even if I found a cave to hide you in, they'd find you, because that's what they do."

"But—" She drew in a breath and let it out. *Say it.* "I trust you to take care of me." And she did. All the way. She managed a small grin. "And you may be unhappy about the gun, but at least I can shoot if I have to."

"I'm not sure if that scares me or reassures me. Besides, we'll have plenty of backup on this. I plan to keep you out of the line of fire."

Still, having that weapon gave her an additional sense of security.

He gave her hand another squeeze but then was silent as they continued to move through the water. Another half hour went by and then Dino steered toward what appeared to be a small uninhabited cove, a place where he could get close enough to drop anchor and…what?

"Why are we stopping here?" she asked.

"Because before we're in the thick of things again, I want us to have a talk and I don't want to be distracted or interrupted. I have a lot of things I should have said years ago and I want to say them now."

"Good things or bad?" she asked, suddenly nervous.

"I'm hoping you'll think they're good."

She had to tamp down the flutters of excitement, but if that kiss earlier was any indication, maybe their relationship was finally going where it should have years ago.

If I hadn't been such a coward and run off.

When the anchor was set and the engine turned off, he took Jen's hand and led her to the cabin below deck.

"Sit," he said. "Please."

She wanted to ask him a million questions, but she sat and waited for him to tell her what was on his mind. And why he was here, although she could pretty much guess that. But first she had something to say herself.

"Before you say anything," she began, "I just want to say again how truly sorry I am that I kept Deanne

from you all these years. It wasn't right. But I just…"
She shrugged, searching for words.

"I get it. You had no reason to think I'd welcome the news."

"So…let's move forward?"

He nodded. "That's what I want, too." He paced across the small area. "I know I wasn't the best bet for a relationship when we were together. My whole life was filled with dangerous activities and having a good time. I guess I figured…" He shrugged. "Looking back, I don't know what I figured. Just that I had a fear of tying myself down. I never bothered to look at the benefits of a relationship. A family. I was a selfish bastard who didn't want strings."

She couldn't help the little smile that crept across her lips. "Oh, you were pretty clear about that."

"I know." He snorted. "I was a real class act. But, Jen, I want you to know I've regretted it every single day since you disappeared. I wish to hell I could turn back the clock and not be such an asshole. I—" He hauled in a breath. "I want you in my life. You and Deanne. And I swear to you, I am going to get you out of this and keep you safe while I am doing it. I swear it on my life."

She was shocked to hear such an emotional declaration from him, but could she believe him?

"Are you just saying that because of what's happened? You feel guilty that I'm in danger?"

He shook his head. "I'm saying it because it's true. My life was empty without you in it, despite all the high-octane adventures. I just wish it hadn't taken you being in danger to get me moving."

"But it did," she pointed out. "Get you moving,

that is. I was pretty sure Ethan would get in touch with you especially because of Deanne. And I hoped that…well…"

His voice was low and steady and even when he spoke again. "Whatever is between us—and I really want us to find out—will take both of us to make it work." He took her hands in his and gave them a gentle squeeze. "And I want that to happen."

She studied him, her gaze intent.

"I'd like that, too," she said at last. "But first you have to understand why I left the way I did and not give me heat about it."

"I think I understand more than you think." He sighed. "Jen, I spent most of my adult life doing extremely dangerous, very intense work for the government. When I lost my parents, I decided fishing was the least stressful thing I could do, which is when Blackwater was born." He was still holding her hands, and he was glad she hadn't tried to pull away. "But I guess that kind of work just naturally heads in my direction. I was approached by the government to handle some off the books situations. Then Ethan went to work for a while at Guardian, and they sometimes need someone to handle a situation that can't hit the agency's records."

"I knew you were involved in dangerous things," she told him, "although you never discussed it, so I never asked."

"Because I couldn't. And we weren't…"

"We weren't in a relationship where you could share anything."

He nodded. "My work was exactly why we weren't in a relationship. I didn't think I had the right to ask anyone to share a life that had a lot of danger woven into it. Where there was always a fifty/fifty chance I might not make it back."

"But if you have feelings for someone," she said slowly, "shouldn't the choice be theirs, too?"

Dino rubbed his face. "Truth? Besides being worried about your reaction, I didn't want to let any of the danger find its way to you. I found it was easier to compartmentalize things and not let myself care too much for anyone."

"That's what you did."

"And too damn well." He huffed out another sigh. "I see now, I looked at it all wrong. I thought if I continued in my line of work, which is what I wanted to do, I couldn't drag anyone else into it with me, because it would put them in danger. And I worried a relationship would damage my focus. I know that's a shit thing to say, but that's what it was. And just maybe I was afraid to open myself up like that to another person. That's the plain, simple truth. But..."

"But?" she prompted, almost holding her breath.

"But I see other people do it and figure out how to deal with the risk. And there is risk," he added, making a point. "Enemies try to get back at people like me by attacking those who are close to us. And Jen, I swear, that's what drove me away from relationships all these years. I wish I'd talked to people, tried to figure out then how to build safety nets."

"Are you sure it wasn't because you liked being unattached and living just as hard as you worked?" she prodded.

Dino ran a hand through his longish hair. "Yes, that, too."

"Or maybe you were just afraid to let yourself get attached to someone. People often see that as a weakness."

She could see him struggling to find the right words. The right answers. *Or did you just not want the responsibility of another person.*

Until now.

"Look. I know I've been an asshole, but when I saw Deanne and realized just how much of her life I'd missed, and how empty it really had been without you in it, I just…" He shook his head, and it was obvious to her he was running out of words.

"And now?" she asked.

When he looked at her face, she saw a mixture of determination and uncertainty in his eyes.

"Now? I know I can't make up for lost time, but I don't want to lose you. Again. Or Deanne. I realized for a long time just how empty my life has been." He raked his fingers through his hair. "I know you don't have one damn reason to believe me, but I want us to make this work, Jen. I swear to god I do."

He only said the L word once, but she was sure more would come. Believed it would because everything he was doing and saying indicated that.

Finally, her mouth curved in a tiny smile, and he seemed to relax just a little. "I want you, too, Dino. Always have. So we'd better figure out how to take care of the bad guys."

He pulled her from the couch where she was sitting and into his arms, giving her a huge hug and a kiss that scorched her body down to her toes. His tongue sought hers, sliding over it, dancing with it, generating more heat. Her nipples hardened, and the walls of her sex pulsed with need. God, she wanted him inside her so badly, filling her with his thick cock, driving her to the most intense orgasms she'd ever experienced.

He slid one large hand down her spine, cupping the curve of her ass and kneading the flesh. His hand was warm, imprinting itself on her flesh through the fabric of her shorts. One thick finger pressed the material into the crevice, sending white-hot flames surging through her.

She wanted to cry out in protest when he moved his hand and lifted his mouth from hers.

"Later," he told her, his voice thick and husky with need and hunger. "Right now, we need to get as far out of the line of fire as we can. And that's just what I'm about to do."

He took her hand and led her back upon deck. She watched as he weighed anchor, kicked over the engines, and pulled out into the Caribbean again. They had a long way to go before this was over, but for the first time in years she felt her life might be moving in the right direction.

Chapter Fourteen

As the private island came into view, Dino cut back on the engines and slowly steered the boat to the private dock and into the available berth. He had insisted Jen go below as they neared the island and told her to stay there until he had a chance to scope things out. Armed or not, he was determined to minimize the danger to her as much as possible.

The trip had been uneventful, thank fuck. He'd taken a couple of detours and monitored the boats around him, but no one changed course to hang on his tail. In fact, the closer they got to their destination, the less water traffic there was. Once he entered the area of all the little private islands, the only boats he saw were those attached to home sites. Two of them headed out to open water as he passed them, but they never turned in his direction.

So far so good. At least he'd be able to tell if any other boats approached.

Leon Fabre, who his client had texted him was the property manager, must have been watching for them because as soon as Dino pulled alongside the dock, he came out of the house to meet them.

"Let me give you a hand," he said as he helped Dino tie up the boat.

"Thanks." Dino jumped down onto the dock and held out his hand, which Leon shook. "I'll do my best not to be a nuisance. I really appreciate your boss allowing me to use the island."

"I'm sure he is happy to be able to repay the huge favor you did for him." Leon smiled. "My orders are to provide anything you might need that we have available."

"You need to make sure you stay out of the way, Leon. We won't be coming into the house at all, but I don't want you in the line of danger."

"No problem." Leon smiled. "As soon as I have you squared away, I'll be taking one of the boats and heading away from here. I'll be gone before the people chasing you even find this place."

"Good. Perfect."

"You are to feel free to stay here for as long as you need," Leon added. "The amenities of the estate are yours to use as you need them, including anything for your boat. And if there is something not available, you are to let me know and we will provide it."

Dino didn't know what to say. He knew the owner was grateful to him, but this was going above and beyond. He wasn't, however, turning anything down if it helped to keep Jen safe.

"I think we're good. But thank you. And please thank your employer."

"One last word. I assume you have no idea when anything will take place—"

"It will most likely be at night. The people looking for us will want to take advantage of the cover of darkness."

"They'll most likely land on the other side of the island if they want to sneak up on you," Leon told them. "There's a small beach there where they can anchor and use an inflatable boat to land or swim in using scuba gear. Be aware. There is also a small waterfall on the other side of the little mountain with a cave behind it. Perhaps you could, um, entice your visitors there. It puts them right in your sites."

He wanted to tell Leon he was hyperaware of more situations than the other man would ever experience but instead he just thanked him.

He waited until Leon headed back to the house, then took his time scanning the area. Since this was the only house on the island, it wasn't as if he had to worry about neighbors. It worried him, however, that as Leon had pointed out on the opposite end of the island there was nothing but thick vegetation and trees. And a small beach. People could indeed approach in SCUBA gear, remove it, and work their way across the island to the house. Probably the best way for Ethan and Blackwater to approach, also.

People like those looking for them had years of experience at stealth, and that in itself was a great danger. But Blackwater was an expert at stealth.

Lifting the binoculars he'd hung around his neck, he scanned as far as he could see in either direction. He hadn't spotted any other boats on the water for at least a half mile, but then he was aware that this area didn't get any water traffic except for visitors to one of the privately owned islands. And he was sure no one would approach until dark.

He hopped back onto the boat and pulled out his cell phone."

"We're on our way," Ethan told him when he answered."

"What about Sutherland and the missing pieces?"

"My source came through for me. Mike's flying a Blackwater backup team to Mexico as we speak. If we're lucky, we'll get there before Welborn's people. If we're not, we'll just pick up the pieces. Either way, we'll make sure word will be out that Jen had no connection whatsoever with this."

Dino blew out a breath. "Thanks for handling this."

"It's what we do."

"I don't expect Dante and his men to land here before dark. And I don't expect they'll be watching this place while it's still too light outside. We've used a number of setups to do this so figure out which one works best and let me know so I'll be ready. We have to time this just right."

"Of course. Talk later."

Dino disconnected and looked at his watch then checked the horizon. By his calculations, they had about four hours before Blackwater arrived and maybe two hours after that, full dark, until Welborn's crew breeched the island. If only he'd been a different person ten years ago, none of this would be happening.

Well, if only didn't get them results, so he'd better get to business.

He climbed down to the main cabin where Jen was waiting for him. It had taken every bit of discipline not to rip off her clothes and lose himself in her the minute he got her on the boat. It felt as if he'd waited forever to be with her again, and with this latest information, impatience was clawing at him. They'd wasted so much time, and now hell was staring them in the face. There wasn't time to rip he a new one for hiding Deanne from him, not if he wanted to move forward with her.

But first, he had things to tell her, things that would

let her know he didn't think the blame was all hers and that he had a burning desire to make up for lost time.

He'd filled a mug with coffee for her before they'd docked, and she was sitting on the couch still holding it. From what he could see, she hadn't had more than a sip or two.

"Is the coffee not good? Too strong? Too weak?" He frowned. "I can make a fresh cup for you."

Not that he gave a fucking crap about the coffee, but he needed props to hold onto his discipline.

She shook her head. "The coffee is fine. I just didn't want to pour any more caffeine into my body until—"

He waited, but when she didn't finish her sentence, he asked, "Until what?"

"Until I have a chance to tell you why I ran away and kept Deanne from you for ten years. That was terrible of me."

All the anger at her disappearance and keeping his daughter secret from him began to dissipate like so much smoke at her words. She looked on the verge of tears, which for Jennifer LaCroix was both unusual and rare. He sat down beside her, relieved her of the cup and set it on the table, and took both of her hands in his.

"Listen to me, Jen." He organized his thoughts as best he could. What he said next was incredibly important. "No one knows better than me what a bad risk I was for fatherhood at that time. For anything."

"But—"

He touched two fingers to her lips. "After my parents were killed, I made a decision not to ever get close to anyone again. The pain of the loss nearly destroyed me. But I told myself, okay, I was alone in the world. No obligations, no one to consider except myself. I could do whatever the hell I wanted. I had work and lots of people I could hang out with. And friends, like Ethan." He paused to draw a breath. "But then Ethan…"

"Met Lisa, fell in love, and got married," she finished for him.

He nodded. "Sometimes, I thought, crap, if Ethan could do a one-eighty with his life, maybe I could, too. But then I'd think, no, what if I mess up?"

"Dino, we all mess up now and then. It's called living."

He snorted a laugh. "If only I'd been smart enough to see it that way. So please don't put this all on your head." He blew out a breath. "I will tell you, when I first found out about Deanne, I was ready to rip your head off for keeping her from me."

"I'm sure you were."

"But then Ethan talked some sense into me. Plus, I've had time now to think about it. I have no idea how you feel about me, but I know how I feel about you. I'm finally able to admit it to myself. When we get out of this mess, I want to make a life with you." When she opened her mouth to speak, he held up a hand. "Let me finish, please, or I might not be able to get it all out."

"Okay." She bit her lower lip, and he didn't know if that was a bad sign or a good one.

"You set the rules, and however you want it, that's what we'll do. I never believed I could let myself love anyone, but Jen? The past few days, it's become very clear to me that not only am I in love with you, but I have been all these years. Shocked the shit out of me, so I want to know. Is there a way we can make this work?"

He held his breath, waiting for her to say something. He hoped like hell the scorching kiss they'd shared meant something more than a prelude to great sex. Finally, she moved closer to him on the couch, placed her palms on his cheeks, and studied his face for a long time, as if reading what she saw there. Then she tilted her head forward and pressed her lips to his, lips that were as soft and warm as he remembered.

Take it slow and easy. Let her take the lead. Don't rush it. Don't make a mistake.

But when she trailed the tip of her tongue over the seam of his mouth, his self-control broke. He cradled her head between his palms and licked her lips with his tongue. When she opened her mouth for him, he thrust his tongue inside and slicked it over every surface.

Heat rushed through him, sizzling his nerve endings, and his cock hardened so much he was afraid it would break the zipper on his fly. Her taste was just as he remembered it, a combination of sweet and spicy and totally erotic. He scraped her tongue with his teeth, giving it a soft bite as he slipped his tongue from her mouth. The moan that whispered from her mouth only made him harder.

God! He just wanted to fuck the hell out of her, for hours and hours.

Sliding his mouth to the right, he placed a string of kisses along her jawline, gently nipped the lobe of one ear, then closed his teeth over the soft flesh. Another moan drifted in the air as she tilted her head to give him better access. He could have kept on kissing her all day, the remembered taste and scent invading his senses, but he wanted so much more.

Sliding his hand around to the front of her body, he eased it beneath the T-shirt she wore until he cupped one breast. He kneaded the mound with gentle squeezes, feeling the hard tip press into the center of his palm. She made the most intoxicating little noises as he molded the flesh to his hand, and he grew impatient with the fabric of her bra acting as a barrier. Shoving it aside, he pinched a nipple between his fingers and tugged on it. Pushing the rest of her bra out of the way, he gave the other breast the same treatment as he had the other, tugging each nipple with his teeth. She arched her back, lifting herself to his mouth.

Jesus!

How had he lived so long without this?

She grabbed his shirt and pushed the material up, up, until he separated himself from her for a moment, allowing her to yank the shirt completely off. Next to go was her T-shirt and lacey bra, until finally their bodies touched flesh to flesh. Banding his arm around her and pressing her close, he took her mouth in another scorching kiss. She thrust her tongue against his, dueling with it, sliding it back and forth. His balls tightened as heat shot through him.

He pulled his mouth from hers, sliding it down so he could take one beaded nipple into his mouth and close his teeth over it. He loved the little noises she made when he grazed his teeth over her breast, teasing first one nipple and then the other.

"Oh! Oh! Oh!"

God!

He loved her fingers digging into his back as he nipped and nibbled. But he needed more. A lot more.

Lowering her onto the couch, he nudged her body

until she was stretched out full length. Forcing himself to take it slow, he unsnapped her jeans and eased them down her legs, tossing them to the side along with her shoes. She lay there wearing only a tiny bikini that barely covered her mound.

Images flashed through his mind, memories of her lying naked on a bed, legs spread wide while he licked every inch of her skin. He wanted that again and he wanted it now.

Dropping to his knees, he shifted her body until he could drape her legs over his shoulders and spread the lips of her sex. Mouth watering at the sight of the pink flesh, he bent forward and took a long, slow lick from top to bottom. Then he did it again, this time taking a moment to flick the tip of his tongue over her clit.

"Mmm." The soft, slow moan drifted from her mouth, and she dug her heels into his back, trying to lift herself closer to him.

She tasted so good, just as he remembered her, a flavor that was a combination of sweet and tangy. And like everything else about her, it went straight to his dick, which was already trying to push its way out of his fly. He drew the tip of his tongue along the wet, pink flesh again and again, finally taking her clit between his teeth and giving it gentle tugs. The sounds she continued to make only ramped up his intense need.

He licked and sucked, driven on by the delicious sounds she made, until that was not enough, and he thrust two fingers into her hot, damp sex.

"Oh, god!" She pressed clenched fists into the couch to stabilize herself as she rode his fingers, back and forth, again and again.

Dino added a third finger, stretching her a little

more and finding that sweet spot that made her cry out. He worked her cunt over and over, driving his fingers again and again until he felt the tremors beginning in her inner muscles. Placing his mouth on her clit he sucked, hard, and she exploded, her sweet juices drenching his tongue.

She had barely finished, her inner walls still clenching, when he rose to his knees and stripped off his clothes. His dick was so swollen he was afraid it might break off, and his balls ached something fierce. He wanted a lot more foreplay. So much more, but he'd given her one orgasm, and he didn't think he could stand much more foreplay without being inside her.

He had presence of mind enough to grab a condom from his wallet—under any and all circumstances he was prepared—and rolled it on with shaking hands. Seconds later he had her fully stretched out on the couch, giving silent thanks that he'd made sure to have a wide one when he bought the boat. He spread her legs and wrapped his fingers around his throbbing cock then eased it into her slick cunt.

Holy motherfucker!

He'd forgotten just how good it felt to be inside Jen, the muscles of her hot, wet channel gripping him like a fist. He felt as if he'd come home after a long journey. He lifted his gaze to look in her eyes, his heart turning over at the hunger and desire blazing there. And something else. An emotion that either hadn't been there all those years ago or that she'd carefully hidden. He was so afraid to give a name to it, and he wanted to laugh at the fact that Don't Give A Damn Dino Brancuzzi was letting his emotions play into this. But it seemed he had no choice, because he couldn't have put his feelings for her back in the box if he'd wanted to.

He drew in a deep breath, let it out slowly, and began to move in and out of her body. She had wrapped her legs around him and dug her heels into the small of his back, locking them together. His movements were slow at first, a steady rhythm increasing in pace. In moments, the familiarity of all those years took over, and they were moving together as if ten years hadn't passed, and they'd just made love yesterday.

Dino did his best to slow himself down, but being inside Jen after so many years was almost too much for him. He almost shouted when the first spasms in her slick walls began to flutter against his cock. He moved faster and harder, doing his best to match his pace to hers.

And then, finally, they were there. Together. Exploding with an orgasm so intense everything else faded away.

He had no idea how long they lay there, joined together, replete but comfortable in their connection. Finally, he lifted his head and looked directly into her eyes, almost afraid of what he'd see there. But whatever he'd worried about, what he saw in her eyes eased his anxiety. His body relaxed, and he rested his head on her shoulder. For a moment, he thought he could stay just like this indefinitely.

Then he remembered that life was not going to wait for them to catch up on their relationship and redefine it. He had people to contact and things to resolve, certainly if Jen wasn't going to spend the rest of her life running from people who wanted to kill her or jail her or whatever turned out to be easiest for them.

He brushed his mouth over hers then smiled. "To

be continued."

She returned the smile. "I hope so." Then she shifted slightly. "Listen, Dino, I—"

"I know. We have a lot of things to work out before we can look at the rest of our lives besides the great sex."

She actually chuckled. "Well, I might not have put it quite that way, but yes. We have a lot of things to straighten out, many of them on my part. I was wrong to just take off the way I did."

He touched the tip of a finger to her mouth. "It wasn't all you. Like I said, we both have a lot of stuff to get through. But we're going to make it, Jen. We're going to, because I want to and I think you do, too. But first we have to get past this mess."

"Agreed."

"And I'd better get rid of this condom before we have a little accident with it."

Pinching the edges of it tight to his cock, he slowly eased from her body and moved toward the bathroom. He stared at himself in the narrow mirror over the sink.

"Don't fuck this up," he told himself. "Do not make a mess out of this. There's nothing to be afraid of. If Ethan can make it work, so can I."

And for the first time, he really believed it.

They were still lying in bed, Jen's head on Dino's shoulder, his arm draped around her, when his cell phone rang. He looked at the readout and saw Ethan's name.

"What have you got?"

"Word that you're in big trouble, but you know that, right?"

"What does that mean?" Dino demanded.

"It means," Ethan told him, "the word is out you have Jen and the two of you are tucked away on that island you think is so secret."

"What?" Dino almost roared the question. "How the hell do they know about this place?"

"Did you pass other boats on the way? Welborn has been spreading money like peanut butter paying for any information on you at all."

"But—"

"I know you've been alert and you watch for everything, but as we both know, even a fishing trawler can be a menace."

He thought back to the boats they passed along the way and could have shot himself. He should have been more diligent, taken a more circuitous route to this island. Anything. He'd really fucked up and put Jen at risk doing so.

"I just got the word that Welborn's men may be within striking distance of her," Ethan said, "and you're going to need all the help you can get protecting her."

"How the fuck did they find where I brought her? No one knows about this island. It's private."

"With people like Welborn and his friends, nothing is secret anymore," Ethan told him, "but at least we can be prepared. Here's what I got from Pizzaro, my contact here in igloo land. And by the way, next time we have to take a field trip, I'm making sure it's south of the Mason-Dixon Line."

"Yeah, yeah, yeah. Come on. Give."

"Welborn's the key. His right-hand man, an asshole named Peter Leneghan, is on the hunt for Jen. When he got no results, he put Dante Fox, the lowest of the lowlifes, sniffing after her."

"Yeah, he was arriving at Hermosa as we left. We barely made it out without being spotted."

"No shit."

Dino wanted to punch someone. He and Ethan could reach out to their own undesirables for specific tasks, but he also knew people like that were dangerous and sometimes uncontrollable. If that was where Welborn was getting his people, his bad feeling about this just got much worse. "What else did you get from Pizzaro?"

"Welborn wants Jen found yesterday, whatever it takes. If she doesn't have the antiquities, if she was just a red herring Sutherland tossed in the mix, then his orders are to kill her."

"Kill her?" Dino's blood turned to ice.

"Uh huh. And the men he has on this would do it without breaking a sweat."

Damn!

"Good thing I already found her." Dino blew out a breath. "Thank fuck for that."

But he still had to find the antiquities and Sutherland. It was the only way to clear Jen's name, thanks to that piece of trash, unless something had changed.

"What about Sutherland? You indicated you had information about him. You know he's my focus. Find him, and we can get to everything."

"Yeah, but I'm telling you," Ethan said, "however this ends, it's going to be a fucking mess. And there's something else in the mix here."

Dino blew out a breath. "Just what in hell would that be?"

"Pizzaro doesn't think Welborn is aware of exactly

how well known his little secret collecting habit is," Ethan told him. "I mean his smuggling arrangement with Sutherland. Or at least how it was before it all blew up in everyone's face. He thinks he had things set up just the way he wanted them, that his little game was totally secret and he had control of it."

"But?" Dino urged.

"But," Ethan said slowly, "in that world, nothing is ever really secret. So people know there's more than the museum board at stake for him here. Welborn now knows Sutherland has all the missing pieces. The minute the man tried to find buyers the word was out everywhere. The news of the missing shipment hit every corner of the dark world. If he can't find Sutherland and those artifacts, he's worried his secret could become public knowledge and he'll lose a lot more than his position as board chairman."

"Hell," Dino swore.

"Yup. He doesn't know it's already out there. Pretty soon there'll be more people after Sutherland than at a football game. But they won't be offering money for those missing pieces. They'll shoot first and then grab the artifacts. Not to mention the FBI is now on his trail and is gathering evidence to land him."

"What a fucked up mess." Dino wanted to hit someone.

"Welborn's desperate, which ratchets up the danger factor. I'm sure he figures if he can find Sutherland, take the smuggled pieces that he paid for and give the rest to the FBI, he can somehow cover over the other shit. And kill Jen just to tie up loose ends. He doesn't want to give up his hobby. This need for those antiquities is like a drug habit with him. "

"So you have an idea where Sutherland is because he's, what, trying to sell the artifacts?" Dino felt a sudden, tiny surge of excitement. Maybe they were getting a break here.

"Let's just say Pizzaro and I put a trail together based on Sutherland's actions the last few days and identified a logical general location. Or locations. Sources are working on being exact right now."

Dino frowned. "How do you know it's him?"

"The few items mentioned came from the list of what was shipped to the museum. Dino, all the sources are verified on this. Every piece of information points to Sutherland."

"So when do you think you'll have an exact location for Sutherland? We've got to lay hands on him. And be sure Jen is protected."

Next to him, Dino felt her body tense. He slid his arm around her and tugged her closer to his side.

"Pizzaro assured me within the next twelve hours," Ethan said. "The people Welborn's got on Sutherland's tail may not be as good as you, but they come pretty damn close, and they aren't giving up a big payday."

"Except he's only interested in getting his toys back," Dino pointed out. "If he gets to Sutherland first, he'll kill him and that does us no good. We have to make sure the world knows Jen was not involved."

"Trust me, Dino, that will be taken care of. But that means you'll need all the help you can get. I know you thought you'd be safely tucked away on that secret island, but like I said, Welborn has his tentacles everywhere and you were spotted. Anyway, you know as well as I do nothing is really secret."

"Jen's the priority," he insisted. "We have to

protect her."

"And we will," Ethan assured him. "We're better than Welborn."

"I'm putting this on speaker so she can hear, too." He punched the button and held the phone so that she could hear

"Ethan, thank you," Jen said. "For everything."

"It's what friends do."

"And are we?" she asked, a hint of uncertainty edging her voice. "Friends?"

"Yes, we are. And when this is all finished, we will celebrate as friends. By the way, I checked with Lisa again this morning and Deanne is doing fine. She misses her mother, but she's really taken to Jamie, and he's kept her busy."

"I don't know how I'll ever thank you. I—" Her voice broke. "Here's Dino."

"You did a good thing, buddy," Dino told him, taking the phone off speaker. "We owe you big time."

"It's not over yet," Ethan pointed out. "But I promise you it will be soon. I have my crew all over this. And another one on Sutherland and the artifacts."

"Keep your crew with you," Dino told him. "We have backup we've used for Blackwater projects that needed a larger team. Run that project through Ben since he's holding down the fort in the office. I'll have him get hold of them and put them on standby for your orders. Mike Hogan will fly them wherever they need to go, and they can handle Sutherland and the artifacts. Jen is our first priority, yours and mine, because she's the one Welborn is the most afraid of."

"So, we'll be backing you up. Period. I'm going to head to Key West with Angel and Octavio. I'm reaching out to them as soon as we hang up. I'll call you when we get there so you can tell us where we're headed."

"You'll need a boat," Dino told him. "I'll call Ben and tell him to get the second Blackwater boat ready for you. Check in with him just before you land."

"Good. Thanks."

"Don't thank me," Dino snorted. "You're the one doing this."

"Okay. We're set. Your assignment is just to stay alert and keep Jen safe."

"I'm on it." He kissed the top of her head. "Believe me."

Chapter Fifteen

Craig Sutherland poured scotch over the ice cubes in the rocks glass and took a healthy swallow. He tried not to think of the fact that he was drinking earlier and more with each passing day. But things were just not going the way he'd expected them to. By now he should have concluded the sale of all the fucking antiquities, so they were out of his possession and the money in a bank in the Cayman Islands. Those first couple of sales had been lucky and beneficial, which was how he acquired the boat he was now sitting in. He had breathed a little sigh of relief. Although he'd worried that making the sales might be a problem, he was relieved when the first couple went so well.

But somehow, between the time he got to Baja with the new boat and the cartons containing the balance of the artifacts, the desire for purchasing them seemed to have taken a turn in the other direction. The people he had put the word out to suddenly were backing away. What was blocking those sales?

It had to be that fucking Welborn. He had contacts everywhere. He could have put the word out that anyone who made a purchase from him was in for trouble. You'd think the kind of people he'd reached out to would tell someone like Welborn to go to hell. Oh, sure, the man was powerful, but so were his prospective buyers. He couldn't imagine any one of them would feel intimidated by Welborn's threats.

Yet here he sat, less than a week after he'd left Michigan, with his treasures locked in a closet on his boat and people avoiding him like the plague.

If only he'd had more sense and less ego. If only he'd recognized his gambling addiction for what it was and been able to do something about it. But he'd been hooked before he realized it. And how stupid, how egotistical had he been to feel so flattered at the invitation to play poker at Roger Welborn's. He might think his position at the museum put him on a level with the people in the game but that was just self-delusion.

And it led him to the mess of smuggling items into the country for Welborn.

He had to make some decisions soon. He was going through his money faster than planned. Paying cash for the boat had eaten a big hole in his bank account, but he hadn't had a choice. Anything else would have left a trail. He was also coming to the conclusion that he might not be suited for permanent boat living.

Well, fuck. I'd better find a way to love it, and pretty damn quick.

He took another swallow of his scotch, silently promising himself to cut way back on it. Then he picked up the extremely expensive cell phone he'd purchased and dialed the man who'd been his contact for the artifacts. Rey Marin operated an import/export company in Brazil that served as a good cover for his under-the-table business. Roger Welborn had always been happy to pay the man's fee on top of the exorbitant cost of the items because Marin was able to get his hands on things others couldn't.

He punched the speed dial and waited impatiently for Marin to answer. It rang five times, unusually longer than normal. He was about to hang up and try again when he heard the man's voice.

"I told you I can't do anything for you."

Sutherland's stomach cramped and he tightened his fist on the phone. "I've made you a lot of money over the years. You owe me."

Marin's laugh was short and sharp. "I owe you nothing. You have brought the wrath of everyone down on us with your greed. Don't call again."

"Wait." Sutherland took a breath. "What do you mean? Why can't I sell these items? They're rarities. You and I both know there are many collectors out there who should be salivating for them."

"Should be is the operative phrase," Marin growled. "Roger Welborn is a power globally. His money funds a lot of things that cannot go through regular channels. Word is out about this, and no one wants to do anything to upset him."

Fuck. Fuck, fuck, fuck.

He certainly hadn't seen this coming. When he'd planned it out, it had all seemed so simple.

"There are still places you can reach out to," Marin told him. "I can give you the names, but they are not people I would do business with. They would kill you and steal the merchandise without a blink of an eye."

"I have to sell them." God, he sounded so desperate.

Silence.

"Let me think about this and see what I can do. But if I arrange something, we split the proceeds fifty-fifty."

Crap. Well, what choice did he have? "Fine. I'll take what I can get."

"Keep your phone on," Marin told him. "I'll call you."

Sutherland stared out the cabin window after hanging up, cursing his rotten luck. He'd probably have to find another place to berth the boat. He wouldn't put it past Marin or anyone he'd come into contact with to locate his signal and rat him out. That could be a problem, too.

And he had to call his wife. Anita had been a real trooper through this, playing the role of the frightened, betrayed wife to the hilt. He wished he had better news to give her, but he was confident if Marin came through, even under the new terms, he'd have enough for them to live comfortably for a long time.

Of course, they'd probably have to change their names, but that was a small matter to accomplish. He knew people. And what the hell did it matter what their names were, anyway?

He checked his watch. He'd told Anita to expect a call early afternoon, but he'd wait a little bit to see if he heard back from Marin. Where they went from here depended almost completely on whether the man had found a buyer for him.

He sighed and wondered if he dared pour himself another drink, wondering if this mess was turning him into an alcoholic.

****

"Peter." Roger Welborn looked at the man sitting across from his desk. "I have to say I'm slightly disappointed in you."

Peter Leneghan looked anything but happy.

"I've got everyone I can reach out to on this," he told his boss. "And I mean everyone. I'm chasing a rumor that he's been seen in Baja California, but the first couple of places on the list were duds. Plus, we are still shaking the trees for black market dealers and collectors, who I hear are suddenly avoiding him like the plague."

"Well, damn it, Peter." Welborn smacked his fist on the desk. "Pretty soon it won't matter. The LaCroix woman and Sutherland will both have disappeared for good along with that whole shipment and I'll be ridiculed by everyone. That doesn't look good for you."

"Twenty-four hours." Leneghan rose from his chair. "Twenty-four hours and you'll have it all. I give you my word."

"I damn well better," Welborn growled. "Now get your ass out of here."

****

Dino was in the cabin of the boat, mentally going over his list, when his phone rang. He checked the readout.

Ethan.

"You on your way?" he asked.

"As we speak. Thanks for making the calls for us."

"Sure. No problem." He had called Mike Hogan and asked him to fly to Michigan, pick up Ethan and his men and ferry them back to Key West. Then he'd called Ben to make sure he was in the loop. Sure enough, Ethan had already called him, and he was getting the boat ready. And finally, Ethan had reached out to Guardian for additional manpower.

"So now we're on our way."

"Excellent. Ben fixed you up?"

"In spades," Ethan assured him. "And we've got every kind of weapon and piece of equipment we could possibly need."

"Ben called us with an update on the boat, and we're good to go. But I wanted to pass along some updates for you."

"Is it about the assholes on our tail?" Dino growled.

"A different asshole. I think I've got news of the location of our absent thief, Sutherland."

Dino's eyes widened. "No shit?"

"No shit at all. We have confirmation that Sutherland does in fact have the missing pieces."

"How the hell did you work that?" he asked.

"Because the idiot left a trail. He managed to sell a few pieces, but the kind of people he did business with would sell their mothers for a dime. Word's all over the place now. He won't be able to unload a fake diamond plus everyone and his brother is headed in his direction."

"Welborn will get to him first," Dino guessed.

"Amen to that. But our other group is headed there just to make sure things get wrapped up properly, the missing pieces don't disappear, and Jen is left out of it completely."

Dino released a breath. "Thank fuck for that. And thank you."

Ethan chuckled. "That's what friends are for. Now. You guys hunkered down there, because we're on our way and not that far from you."

"Ethan, seriously, thank you. I—"

"Hey. You've saved my ass enough times over the years. I'd never have gotten Lisa and Jamie out of the

Quintana Roo if not for you and your guys. So call this even, at least for now."

Dino knew that friends like Ethan were practically nonexistent. He had to swallow twice before he could speak. "I owe you, buddy."

"We'll talk about that later. I'm going to radio you updates as we get closer. You still have that secure channel that can't be hijacked?"

"I do." Dino rattled off the frequency.

"Good deal. See you on the flipside. Caine over and out."

Chapter Sixteen

Dino triple checked the sensors he'd set up on the outside of the boat. They could detect movement within a fifty-foot perimeter of anything over fifty pounds. He hadn't wanted to be busting his ass checking every fucking fish that swam near him. He would have liked something that set a wider perimeter, but at the moment there didn't seem to be anything available. At least this would send him signals of any approaching boat and give him plenty of warning where he'd be hiding with Jen.

Checking once more that everything was in order, he went down to the cabin where Jen was waiting for him. God. Every time he laid eyes on her now, he just wanted to rip her clothes off and fuck her senseless. He was having a huge problem keeping his dick in his pants and at rest.

He clicked off, but instead of putting the phone back in his pocket, he placed it on the low table in front of the couch. He was losing the battle raging inside him, the conflict of the need to deal with what was at hand versus the need to make up for ten years of his stupidity. Because it was on his shoulders.

They had a tiny bit of breathing room, and he planned to use every second of it, although it would take him forever to make up for all the lost time. He stared at her for a very long moment, at the face that had haunted his dreams all this time. Without uttering another word, he eased Jen back against the arm of the couch. Her eyes widened in surprise, her mouth opened slightly, and Dino slid his tongue right in.

He wove his fingers into her hair, clasping the back of her head as he ran his tongue over every inner surface of her mouth. Bang! It was akin to a rocket going off between the two of them. The kiss was so incendiary, it seared her lips. The gentle pressure became firmer, and his tongue came out to stroke her lower lip, and she opened for him as if it was the most natural thing in the world.

Heat shot through him, and his cock threatened to explode. He bit her tongue gently, then sucked it hard into his mouth.

Jen's quick response stunned him. He'd hoped and prayed it hadn't weakened, or that everything going on hadn't changed it. This was even better. When everything was taken care of and they were free of the assholes, the relationship between them would be better than ever and the sex would be through the roof. Even with danger looming over them, his heart did a happy flip.

She wriggled down until she was almost lying flat, with his body on top of her, pushing her hips upward and rubbing her body against his shaft. He dragged his mouth down the line of her neck, taking little nips as he did so then licking the bite marks. The little moans drifting from her lips upped the heat factor a thousand degrees.

He was impatient this time, not willing to go slow. That was for next time, once he'd slaked this hunger raging through him.

Sliding a hand beneath her T-shirt, he cupped one firm breast and squeezed it gently, loving the way it fit so nicely in his palm. He tweaked the hard nipple through the soft fabric of her bra, his cock twitching at her sigh of passion. He eased his hand to the other breast, the other nipple, and gave them the same treatment, but it wasn't enough. She was writhing beneath his touch, and the sounds she was making made his balls ache.

Lifting himself from her body, he tugged her T-shirt over her head, unhooked her bra, and tossed it to the side. The sight of her naked breasts and those dark rose plump nipples was enough on its own to make him come in his jeans. He feasted on her nipples, sucking and licking and biting until her moans blended into one long heated sound. Then he trailed kisses all over the upper body while she writhed beneath him, pressing herself against him while his cock swelled and throbbed.

Sliding off the couch, he knelt beside it stripped off the rest of Jen's clothing, and positioned her so he was kneeling between her thighs. He reached for every bit of self-control, wanting to make this as good as possible. Then he pried open the lips of her cunt and treated himself to a long, slow lick of her slick pink flesh. He had to swallow the moan that slid up his throat at the taste of her.

Using his shoulders to keep her thighs separated he nibbled on her clit, tugging it with his tongue before lapping away at it. He slid it into the hot channel of her pussy, tasting her sweetness before replacing his tongue with two fingers. She gasped and hitched her hips toward him, and he began to fingerfuck her in earnest.

And her cries of pleasure only aroused him more.

He wanted his dick inside her more than he wanted his next breath, but first he wanted to make her come with his mouth again and his hands. Adding a third finger, he filled that hot wet channel and began a hard, steady rhythm. At the same time, he lightly closed his teeth on her throbbing clit and tugged and nibbled.

"Oh, oh, oh."

She hitched her hips at him, riding his hand and his mouth. He slid his tongue over her clit and pulled it between his lips. With a cry, she exploded, spilling herself onto his hand while he drove his fingers in and out. Her inner walls spasmed against them as her orgasm went on and on until the last tremor subsided.

He sprinkled kisses on her inner thighs, up over the curve of her pussy, and up her body to her mouth.

"Taste yourself on me." His voice was rough with hunger. "You taste so good. I'm never going to lose that taste again."

She drew in a breath and let it out slowly. "I don't even know what to say." She threaded her fingers into his hair and held his head so they were looking eye to eye. "I want you to be sure, because there's so much at stake here."

"Sweetheart, I am sure. Positive. No wiggle room." He cupped her cheeks. "You can bet on that."

He held his breath waiting to see if she trusted him or not or was afraid that what she probably thought of as the real Dino would suddenly appear. At the point where he was about to accept that he'd waited too long, she nodded.

"Okay. Let's say we start from this day forward. When we're out of this mess…"

"When we're out of this mess we're going to pick up Deanne, I'm going to show both of you I have what it takes to be a great father and husband, and we're going to build a life together." He brushed a soft kiss over her mouth. "Now let's get you dressed. Ethan will be here soon."

She frowned. "But what about you? Don't you get to be satisfied, too?"

He grinned. "It will give me incentive to get this over with and done." He stood up and reached out a hand. "Come on. I'm going to make fresh coffee. I think we'll need it."

****

Roger Welborn dropped two ice cubes into the rocks glass on his credenza and poured two fingers of Pappy Van Winkle into it. He kept a small bar in his office for clients when a situation needed soothing or celebrating. He hoped today he'd finally have something to celebrate. The past week had stretched his nerves to the breaking point.

The media was giving the disappearance of the artifacts much more press than he thought they should. Maybe it was a slow week for news. He had just finished a call from the vice chairman of the board who "suggested" they call an emergency board meeting. Donors were all up in their grill, the bad publicity was hurting the museum, and they didn't seem to be any closer to a resolution than they had a week ago.

"Twenty-four hours," he'd told the woman. "The FBI is hot on their trail, and I have outside sources working on it, too."

"Outside sources? Why don't I, and the rest of the board, know about it?"

He ground his teeth.

"Because I didn't want to say anything until I knew for sure they were on the trail. If too many people knew, word could get out and we'd lose any advantage." He ground his teeth. "But I promise to have something tomorrow and have my secretary get everyone together."

"We have to," she insisted. "You can't leave the board in the dark like this."

"Understood."

What he really wanted to do was leave the board in the dark for everything. Find that asshole Sutherland and hope he had the missing pieces. Grab most of them, keeping a few for himself, kill Sutherland and Jen LaCroix, and return everything else to the museum without anything splashing on his shoes.

"Roger, I'm going to assume that you have people working on this that none of us know. Perhaps people you use in your international dealings? The kind we all know you have but never discuss?" Her sigh was audible. "If they can resolve the problem, then no harm, no foul. But you must call a board meeting and tell us something."

"How about four o'clock tomorrow?" he asked. "I'll have my secretary contact everyone. And we'll have it at my club, away from the media and other prying eyes."

The pause was infinitesimal. "Fine. I'll look forward to that call."

He carried the drink back to his desk and sipped at it until he felt his nerves settle again.

He picked up his cell phone and was about to call Dante Fox when the phone rang and the readout showed him it was the man himself.

"I hope to hell you've got something for me," he snarled, "because this mess just keeps getting bigger."

"More than you could hope for. We've got everyone's location. I have a team on the way to where Brancuzzi thinks he's got Jen safely hidden and Hammer has another one headed to Baja California."

Welborn tamped down the excitement that surged through him.

"And you're positive of the location?"

"Yes," Fox assured him. "I want the payday you promised."

"Good work, then. Do me a favor. Get Leneghan dialed into Baja."

And I don't want to lose him. He's loyal and still does good work.

"Whatever you want. I'm on it."

"I want updates," he insisted.

"I'll get you what I can, but they can't stop what they're doing to send messages," Fox pointed out.

"Figure out a way."

Welborn disconnected the call. He was doing his best to hold onto his excitement. He'd been in situations like this before where he'd thought success was right at his fingertips, only to have it snatched away by events over which he had no control.

He was still sitting there, thinking of all the things that could possibly go wrong when his phone rang again. He looked at the readout. Leneghan.

"Are you planning to cut me out of everything?" Leneghan snapped when he answered. "This is bullshit. I carry your water for ten years, sometimes in a very leaky pail, and you bring in Fox and Hammer and blow me off?"

Welborn had been expecting this. Leneghan was, of course, only human.

"I'm not cutting you out at all. But I felt time was short here, and we needed all the help we could get. In fact, Hammer has located Sutherland's hideaway and will be calling you shortly with details."

"He damn well better," Leneghan spouted. "I've also had feelers out to see who, if anyone, is buying the missing pieces. I don't know if your other guys have discovered this, but Sutherland has only been able to get rid of a couple of items. This is such a fucking mess the usual buyers are hands off. He's really had to reach out to try and set up sales."

"I just recently learned that. In fact, I was getting ready to call you about it right now."

Liar! But he needed Leneghan, and the man was, after all, a loyal employee.

"I haven't—Wait. I have a call coming in right now. You'd better hope that's him. Let me take it and call you back."

"Do that."

There was just so much that could go wrong with this whole debacle. If Sutherland was standing before him, he'd have a hard time not killing the man. He blew out a breath and took another sip of his drink. He had to keep himself under control. People might be speculating that he had some involvement, but for the moment, there was no proof. He was going to do his best to keep it that way.

****

Dino had stocked the boat with all the basics, including food, so in the context of the situation, he and

Jen had what they needed.

"You need to eat something while we're waiting," Dino told her. "All you've had today is a muffin and enough coffee to float this boat. I don't care if you say you've lost your appetite. You need to keep up your strength. Those jackasses may not be able to find us before Sutherland's captured and the missing pieces retrieved, but we can't take that chance."

She sighed. "I'll do my best. It's just that my stomach's tied up in a big knot."

"I can understand that." He grinned, easing her tension a tiny bit. "I have a surefire way to handle that, but I think, from now on, that's going to have to wait until this is all wrapped up." The grin faded. "I need all my resources focused on protecting you, no matter how appealing anything else is."

"I know." She shook her head. "What a mess. Whoever thought that working in a museum and staying off the radar would end up like this?"

"Come here." He held out his arms, and she walked into them, pressing herself against his hard chest as he wrapped those arms around her.

"I wish I could take back the last ten years," she told him, and really meant it.

"If only wishing made things so. But you know what they say. Everything happens for a reason."

She swatted his chest. "I wish I knew who they are. Maybe they could tell me why the hell this is happening."

Maybe if she'd had the guts to stay and talk to him…

"Stop that." His voice cut into her thoughts. "Whatever you're thinking, stop it right now.

Everything happens for a reason may sound trite, but I'm coming to believe it. Don't play the What If game, Jen. What's done is done. We're given another chance here. I say let's make the most of it."

She wrapped her arms around him and pressed herself against the hard-muscled wall of his chest. If only she could stay here, just like this, forever. But he was right. They were being given an unexpected second chance, and they needed to make the most of it.

"It's okay, babe. We both made bad choices, but we have a second chance. I for one say, let's grab it and hold on." He tilted her face up so she was looking directly into his eyes. His head lowered, and she prepared for his kiss, but his cell rang.

The readout showed Ethan's number so he put it on speaker.

"What do you have for me?" he asked.

"I have bad news and good news," Ethan told him. "Which do you want first?"

"Let's have the bad, first."

"Okay. The bad news is a boat about the size of yours is on the way to where you and Jen are on La Cascada. My sources tell me it's about two hours out."

"Motherfucker." He clenched his jaw. "Well, as soon as we found out who the people were Welborn had reached out to we knew it was a possibility."

"The better news is," Ethan told him, "Blackwater One is only about a half an hour from you, so we've got a lead on them. The even better news is a Guardian chopper just landed Nick and two of his agents on this boat, so we've got a full crew coming in for you. But we can't beat these motherfuckers on the water. My suggestion is you get the fuck off that boat. I think you're too much of a sitting duck the way you are, and you need this whole crew backing you up. Does that island you're at have a lot of cover on it?"

"It does," Dino answered.

Every muscle in Jen's body tightened. All kinds of dangerous possibilities were running through her mind, but Dino had told her all about Blackwater. She knew if anyone could get them out of this it was them. Blackwater.

She had faith that Dino would get them out of this. It seemed he could do just about anything. She believed in him, much more with every minute. But this was the nitty gritty real bad guys. She didn't want them to be killed just when they'd figured out they wanted to build their lives together with Deanne. A strong future as a family.

Okay, he can do this. Just keep believing in him.

And Ethan, and all their friends, even the ones she didn't know. The people after them were dangerous killers, but she'd come to realize from their conversations and what she'd overheard that Dino and Ethan could be more dangerous than anyone else. She'd just trust them. That's all.

"Okay," Dino said. "I'm going to get Jen off the boat here right away. You have your radio?

"I do."

"Okay. I'm getting us to the far side of the island. There's a tiny landing beach there and good natural concealment. Have you guys got the proper equipment so you can make shore there? We don't know for sure where Fox and his men will come ashore so we have to be prepared for anything."

Ethan snorted. "Does a dog wag its tail? I may not

be actively involved in this part of the business anymore, but I keep my skills sharp."

"Okay, okay. Just checking. Get going." Dino looked at Jen reassuringly. "We'll arrive in approximately an hour, just at the edge of darkness."

"We'll be waiting."

Jen watched, fascinated. She had only known the man in a social situation, so seeing him in mission mode was a real revelation to her. He certainly kept himself in top condition. When they were naked in the cabin of the boat, her mouth had watered at the sight of his muscular, lean, ripped body. There were scars that disturbed her, and sometime, she would ask him about them. But he was here and alive and taking care of her, and right now, that was what was important.

She'd lost her appetite for the rest of the sandwich, even though Dino had urged her to eat as much as she could.

"We won't get another chance for a long time," he reminded her. "By then we'll be celebrating our happy ending."

"Is it going to be?" She studied his face. "A happy ending?"

"Absolutely. Come on. I'm going to get our gear ready."

****

"Time to move." Dino shoved his cell phone in his pocket. "Ethan just called and said they're about an hour out."

He led Jen off the boat and hefted the canvas bag with his Sig Sauer, a Beretta M9, and an M4A1 rifle packed in it. Then he checked that his KA-BAR knife was secure in its holster at his ankle and that he had enough ammunition for all the weapons including Jen's. He also added two bottles of water. He was treating this like any other mission.

Using the binoculars around his neck, he scanned the horizon in all directions. All the lights were off at the house. In the opposite direction, two sailboats bobbed in the distance. When he was satisfied they were as clear as possible, he led her up the steps toward the house. But then he curved around to the right on a path that led into the thick jungle of trees and tropical shrubs.

"Watch your step," he cautioned. "Don't step on one of these exposed roots. It's easy to twist your ankle. And these exotic bushes, some of them have branches that can scratch."

She managed a tiny laugh. "Now you tell me."

For the rest of the way, they walked in silence until suddenly a roaring sound filled the air. Jen stopped and tugged on Dino's arm.

"What? We have to keep moving."

"What's that sound?"

"The waterfall. La Cascada. It's what the island's named for. Leon says there's a cave behind it if we need a place to hide, but I'm hoping we can take care of these guys without needing that."

"Um, well, yeah. Me, too."

"Come on. Not much farther."

He was glad when they reached the beach. It was short and narrow, just as he'd been told, but the bushes were so thick it was easy to conceal themselves. He got Jen settled, made sure all the weapons, including hers, were properly loaded, placed all but the Sig Sauer on top of the canvas bag, and hunkered down to wait. He constantly monitored what was happening on the water and the feed from the radar on the boat.

His cell phone rang, and Ethan's voice growled at him. "We're ready to dive."

"Don't tell me that includes you, old man," Dino teased. Then he remembered how impressed he'd been with Ethan's physical condition when he saw him a few days ago. For all he knew, the man trained with his classes.

"Don't worry about me. You just make sure to hold up your end. This is split second timing."

"We're good," Dino assured him.

He disconnected and stuck the phone in his bag. He had one last thing to say before he stepped back into mission mode. He took one of Jen's hands in his and gave it a gentle squeeze. "When this is over, we're going to talk about the future. For the three of us. I want one, and I hope you do."

When she didn't say anything at first, he could have shot himself for bringing this up now, but he wanted her to know how he felt.

"I do," she said at last. "Dino, I shouldn't have run away like I did, but—"

"But you only saw me as a high-octane asshole looking for a good time. And you weren't entirely wrong, so a heavy load of the blame falls on my shoulders. But I'm going to fix that as soon as we're done here. Then we're going to create a new life together. Count on it."

"I look forward to it." Her smile sent heat surging through his body. "To being with you. And Deanne."

He lifted her hand and kissed her knuckles. "So let's get this done."

Chapter Seventeen

When Welborn's cell phone rang, he snatched it up and pressed the button to answer. "What the fuck is going on? You're supposed to call me with updates."

"I said I would when I have any," Dante Fox reminded him. "Fortunately, I do have something."

"Let's hear it, and it better be damn good news."

"We're close to getting them," Fox told him. "In fact, we're almost there."

Welborn felt a spurt of savage pleasure as the words registered, but then he realized a lot was missing. "What do you mean close? Where are you? And which of them? The woman? Sutherland? And how close?"

There was a slight pause.

"Both of them," Fox amended. "We should have our hands on them shortly."

"Fucking shit, Fox," Welborn exploded. "If you don't have hands on them, you don't have them at all."

"Not true. The LaCroix woman is on a private island that we are less than thirty minutes away from. Five minutes after that she's ours."

"Is she by herself?" Welborn wanted to know.

"Unfortunately, no."

"And Sutherland?" Welborn demanded.

"Rey Marin, your good friend who finds those off the books artifacts for you, is helping him find buyers for this phantom shipment. Converts the goods to cash."

"*My* cash," Welborn slammed his fist on the desk. "I want this mess cleaned up at once."

"Roger, I've been asking a lot of questions to get the results you want. Just in case you're interested, it appears Jennifer LaCroix had absolutely nothing to do with this. Sutherland used her as a red herring."

"That bastard." Rage surged in his throat. "How close are you to retrieving my artifacts?"

"Less than thirty minutes," Fox assured him. "Leneghan hooked up with us, and we're setting up the takedown right now. He's got a couple of ragged-looking bodyguards that he probably scraped off the street. No sweat. We just need to make sure there aren't any booby traps before we move in."

"Well, get it done. I want that shipment and I want it now, before the Feds find out where it is and the museum gets it."

"I hear you."

"Tell me again where LaCroix is?"

"On a small private island. The guy that owns it must be a friend of Brancuzzi's. We can't find anything that indicates ownership. My guess is he thinks they're all but invisible there and he can keep her stashed until this all blows over."

"And you're sure he's alone with her? From what you told me about him, that doesn't seem very smart."

"Even the smartest of us get caught in situations now and then," Fox told him. "Not to worry. I have a crew on the way. We'll hit the island after dark and get the job done."

"The next time I hear from you," Welborn snapped, "I want to know Sutherland and LaCroix are dead and you have all the missing pieces. I want pictures of their bodies and of the artifacts. Then I'm going to find a place to live well for the rest of my life and slowly destroy the rest of my enemies. Keep that in mind."

****

Jen was glad Dino had found a flat rock for her to sit on where she was sheltered by the thick greenery. He'd handed her night vision goggles and showed her how to set them, then hung another pair around his neck. Neither of them was visible from the water, but he had managed a tiny opening in the jungle-like growth where he had an unobstructed view of the water and the beach. He had asked Leon to turn out all the lights, both inside and out, so the island was shrouded in darkness. The only illumination came from the moon and was reflected on the calm surface of the water.

She was fascinated to see how still he sat, focused on what he was doing, not distracted by anything, yet totally aware of all the sounds around them. The darkness was peppered with calls of night birds, and behind that, she could hear the muted roar of the waterfall. If the situation hadn't been so dangerous, the setting might even be romantic.

Ethan had given them a thirty-minute warning. She'd tried counting off the minutes in her head, and just when she thought she'd reached the last one, little ripples appeared on the surface of the water. Then one head appeared, covered in scuba headgear, then another and soon there were six men headed to shore. One of them carried a waterproof bag about the size and shape of a small duffel. Slowly and quietly, they emerged from the water and made their way onto the tiny beach. As they stripped off their wet suits and gear, Dino rose and went to meet them.

They shook hands all around and spoke in soft tones. Then Dino turned and motioned her to come forward.

"Good to see you again, Jen," Ethan told her, shaking her hand.

"I was afraid you'd never speak to me again after the way I left."

"We all have our reasons for what we do. By the way, your daughter is doing great. Jamie's taking good care of her, and Lisa's teaching her to bake cookies."

"Thank you so much for doing this."

"It's what friends do," he told her.

She was introduced to Angel and Octavio, and then to Nick Vanetta who introduced her to the two Guardian agents. After that, there was no talking. Guns and ammo were distributed to everyone while scuba and wet suits were rolled up tightly and stuffed at the base of a very thick bush.

"Is it okay to leave them there?" Jen asked

"They can't be seen unless you're looking for them," Angel pointed out, "and we'll get them when we're finished."

"We're going to the waterfall," Dino told them. "I'm going to assume they'll check the boat first, just in case we're stupid enough to wait for them there. Then the house, where they'll find nothing. Then they'll start to search the island. Everything leads back to the waterfall, and we can wait there. According to the map of the island my client sent me, it's the best spot for an assault. Which is what we are definitely going to do."

"Lead on," Ethan told him.

"This way." Dino took Jen's hand and tugged her

directly behind him, then headed through all the greenery toward the roar of the cascading water.

Nick was right behind them, with the rest of the men falling in line. As they got closer, the roar grew louder, and Jen wondered how they'd even hear someone approach. But the men didn't seem bothered by it, and the waterfall was beautiful. It seemed to spill from the top of a high rocky wall, cascading into a pool below, the water then running into a cave. The moon shone down on the scene, its rays reflecting off the water. Jen thought how gorgeous it was and how terrible that its beauty was being disturbed by criminals.

Dino led her behind the actual cascade of water. Then he and Nick huddled with the others over the map on Dino's phone while they figured out the best places for everyone. Once it was decided, the men stationed themselves in strategic positions. They all wore night vision goggles, and Dino signaled Jen to put hers on. Weapons were checked, and then there was nothing to do but wait.

Jen had no idea how the men picked up the faint sounds that they did, but just when she wondered if the invaders were going to show, Dino shifted and pointed in the direction of the house. Standing behind the waterfall made it hard for Jen to hear, but straining, she finally made out voices from the direction of the boat.

Dino came around to where she was standing and put his mouth close to her ear. "As soon as they search the house, they'll head this way, figuring we're hiding in the middle of the island. That's what they would do. Get your weapon ready."

Jen took the Sig Sauer from the holster and checked the load, noting the other men grinning at

Dino. Then she was ready.

"You stay in the cave entrance," he told her, "and hold your position."

"Got it," she acknowledged.

She had no idea how much time passed again, but with her NVGs on she saw the four men take up positions at the edge of the waterfall. It was easy for them to see the path she and Dino had taken from the house, and she could hear whoever was on the island moving along that same path.

A tall man holding a rifle emerged from the greenery, then turned to look at someone behind him. "I'd bet money they're hiding somewhere here by the waterfall," he said. "Let's see if we can flush them out."

He pointed his rifle just past the cascade and began spraying bullets in a circle. As soon as the man with the rifle began shooting, she heard shots from her right and the man fell to the ground.

"Fuck," someone said, and more bullets began to fly.

Even with the NVGs, she couldn't see Dino or Nick or Ethan or any of the others, but she could hear them. She heard the crashing of underbrush and the crack of bullets, but she had no idea who was hit. She edged slightly forward so she was standing at the edge of the pool where the water landed, the cascade roaring in her ears.

"Well, that wasn't smart," she thought when she realized it diminished her hearing ability.

She started to move back when a strong arm circled her neck.

"Don't make one move," a voice said. "I thought there was a hiding place back here. Glad my men kept your people busy, so I could get back here. Drop your gun, and I won't shoot you in the head."

She could scream, but she had no idea whether anyone would hear her with the roar of the water. She dropped the gun, then flinched as he ripped off the NVGs. The man frog-marched her to the front of the cascade where two bodies lay on the ground and a third man was on his knees, Dino standing with a gun to the man's head.

"Drop it," the man behind her said.

Dino turned to where they were, a look of pure rage on his face. "If you kill her, you won't get off this island alive."

Jen shivered at the ice in his tone.

Ethan and Nick were nowhere in sight.

"Oh, I'm keeping her alive until I get out of here. And I'm keeping the gun to her head. If you shoot me, my finger will probably pull the trigger."

Jen saw Angel off to the side, slowly circling toward the back of the area. Octavio stood near Dino. She was sure they wouldn't make a move until the gun was no longer held to her head. But these men had handled situations like this before, and she prayed they'd find a way to free her. What if they got shot doing it? All the emotions of the past few days, the anger over the situation at the museum, the rage at Craig Sutherland's stupidity and his selfishness and pointing the finger at her, the greed of Roger Welborn who had put this whole thing in place came welling up.

She waited for the moment when her captor started to move her forward and the second when his arm around her neck would loosen slightly. The second it did, she grabbed it, sinking her teeth into his arm. When he jerked it back, she bent over and jabbed her elbow into his balls. Then she dropped to the ground and rolled to the side.

At the same time, a shot rang out. She turned her head, afraid of what she might see. Instead of any of the Blackwater/Guardian team being injured, her captor lay on the ground, doubled over, blood seeping from a wound in his shoulder.

In seconds, Dino was beside her, lifting her from the ground and holding her so tightly she almost couldn't breathe. "Fuck, Jen, you scared ten lives out of me."

Then, despite the critical nature of the situation and the men all watching, he cupped her head, drew her mouth to his and kissed the life out of her.

"We must be losing our edge," Ethan said in disgust, "to let that guy get behind the waterfall."

"That's not it," Nick told him. "He hung back from the others he was with, and while we were busy taking care of them, he worked his way around to you. Lesson learned."

Dino ended the kiss and helped her around the waterfall to the place where Angel and Octavio were standing over three bodies. Ethan dragged the man who'd been her captor to his feet, yanking his hands behind him, and using extra strength to aggravate the wound in his shoulder.

"Well, we need to clean up this mess here," Dino said, yanking his cell from a pocket. "Good thing I know the authorities in this area."

"Yeah, let's get this taken care of," Ethan remarked. "And we'd better check in with the crew that's after Craig Sutherland and the artifacts."

"My team is there," Dino said. "My team leader just texted me they have it under control and to call when I can."

Jen leaned against Dino's hard chest.

"Does this mean it's over?" she asked.

"Almost," he said. "We just have to clean up a few loose ends. Then we can talk about the rest of our lives."

Chapter Eighteen

"Is it really you?"

They were still on the boat, heading north from the island.

"Yes, honey, it's me." Jen held Dino's cell tightly in her hand, swamped with relief at the sound of Deanne's voice. "And I'm on my way home. At last."

"To Ethan and Lisa's?"

"Yes. And then to our own home. Wherever we decide it should be."

She could hardly wait to hug her daughter and kiss her sweet face.

"Is...is, um, Dino coming with you? Lisa said he has a special story to tell me."

Jen laughed even as tears rolled down her cheeks. "Yes, he is, and I hope you love the story."

"Then let's get going," Dino said in her ear.

It had taken the better part of two days to work with the authorities to clean up the mess at La Cascada. Dino hadn't wanted there to be any blowback on the man who had lent him the use of the island, and the authorities, well aware of the man's influence, were most accommodating.

Jen had called Lexie to tell her what had happened and apologize for running off without a word. She promised that she and Dino and Deanne would come to Hermana shortly and spend some time with her after this was far enough in the past and their lives were in some kind of normal.

Although much of the rest of the work, such as the mess at Baja California, was handled by the other Blackwater team, Dino was still in control. Fortunately, with his connections and Ethan's, they were able to tie up any loose strings. The Guardian helo retrieved Nick and his two agents and choppered them back to San Antonio.

Now it was early evening, two days later. Mike Hogan airlifted Ethan, Dino, and Jen and deposited them at Ethan's house.

Mike never even turned off the helo, planning to return at once to Key West, but as Dino was about to leave the helo, Jen saw Mike grab his arm.

"You hit the jackpot this time," she heard him tell Dino. "Don't fuck it up."

Dino smiled. "I don't intend to, but you could wish me luck anyway."

Lisa had walked out of the house and stood on the back patio, waiting for them. As Ethan swept her into a kiss that singed the air, Dino put his arm around Jen and pulled her close to his body.

"I want that," he told her. "With you." He pressed his mouth to her ear. "Will you take a chance on me?"

She turned to look at him and smiled. "I think we might be able to work that out."

Dan Mora was also standing there. He shook hands with both Ethan and Dino.

"Everything is in good shape," he told them. "No problems at all."

"We all really appreciate this," Ethan told him. "Thanks so much. For everything."

"You've got a great setup here, Ethan. I told Nick when I'm back in the office I have some suggestions as to how Guardian can use it. There's never a point in this business where you don't need training."

Ethan grinned. "Thanks. Tell him I'll be sure you get the friends and family discount."

Then Dan was gone, and Lisa was waving everyone in through the back door.

"Come on. Come in," she urged. "You have two very eager and anxious kids who are about to explode waiting for you." She looked at Jen and Dino. "One of them as nervous as she is excited."

Jen had talked to Deanne for a long time on the phone while she was waiting for Dino and Ethan to finish their business. It was hard explaining to her why for ten years she'd perpetuated the myth that she chose not to tell Dino about her because he led a dangerous life, and she did not want to bring Deanne into that environment. It was equally difficult explaining because Dino insisted she put the call on speaker so he could listen. And also participate when needed. Deanne had so many questions, which Jen did her best to answer, but it was obvious Deanne was both angry and hurt. They'd have a lot of explaining to do and a lot of fences to mend to make this all work.

But Dino was insistent that he wanted this, and he tried his best to make her believe that. He wanted to marry her, and he wanted his name on Deanne's birth certificate. Somehow, she'd have to get that done. It helped that he took every opportunity to tell her he loved her. That he knew he'd love Deanne, and that he wanted them to make up for the ten lost years.

As they walked into the kitchen, he took her hand

and squeezed it, probably as much for himself as it was for her. They stopped where Jamie and Deanne stood, holding hands, Deanne looking nervous and Jamie looking fierce, as if he'd defend her forever, so much like Ethan.

Jen let go of Dino's hand and held her arms out to Deanne, who, after a moment, ran to her and hugged her as hard as she could. Jamie, after watching to make sure Deanne was okay, hugged his father, hard.

"I'm glad you're my dad," he said, his tone almost a whisper but loud enough that the adults could hear it.

"Ditto in spades," he told the boy.

"Why don't we all sit down at the table," Lisa suggested. "I have coffee, juice, hot chocolate and fresh cupcakes."

"Damn." Dino eyed the food. "Count me in for the cupcakes."

But Jen was pleased to see, before he took one for himself, he put one on a small dessert plate and set it in front of Deanne. The moment had been filled with emotion when Jen told the little girl that Dino was her father, and they were still finding their way through the emotional minefield.

"You like chocolate cupcakes?" he asked Deanne.

She nodded and watched him carefully for a few minutes before she took a bite.

By the time the cupcakes had been devoured, along with the hot chocolate with whipped cream that Lisa served, Jen could see that Deanne's tension had eased slightly, but she and Dino needed to have a long and difficult talk with Deanne. First, they needed to fill Lisa in on how things had wrapped up.

Jamie and Deanne were persuaded to go to the

game room with a promise that Jen and Dino would be talking to Deanne very soon.

"Okay." Lisa sat at the table with her own cup of coffee after serving everyone else. "I want details. Now."

"It was a big mess," Ethan told her. "No exaggeration. Okay, Sutherland first. Welborn learned his location about the same time we did and sent men after him. The missing artifacts were in his Baja California rental, and Welborn wanted them. But Dino sent a second Blackwater team who dispatched Welborn's men and grabbed up the missing pieces."

"Which were then put on a private plane and flown to Michigan," Dino added, "and personally escorted to the museum."

Lisa frowned. "But who was there to accept them? Surely not Welborn and I'm assuming Sutherland is locked away in someone's jail."

Jen nodded. "Absolutely, and no one is happier than me. The vice chairman of the board is handling things temporarily, but they have a lot of work to do."

Lisa nodded. "I'm sure. And Welborn's men who were there?"

"Either being patched up at a hospital or in temporary quarters at a jail in Baja awaiting their personal escorts from the FBI," Dino said. "Welborn and Sutherland are also current guests of FBI hospitality."

"And the men who attacked you at La Cascada."

"Taken care of," Dino told her. "They won't be bothering anyone anymore, although we did leave one in shape to talk."

"So everything's wrapped up?" she asked.

"Yes." Jen was the one who answered. "Done. Finished." She glanced at Dino who nodded. "Time to move on."

"And time for us to talk to a little girl," Dino added. "One who needs to know her family life is going to get a lot better real fast. So if you both will excuse Jen and me, I think important business awaits us."

****

Two days later, Dino, Jen, and Deanne waited on the Caines' back patio while Mike Hogan once again landed his helicopter in the back yard.

Jen had been thrilled that, after the initial awkwardness, Dino and Deanne had become comfortable with each other and a good relationship was slowly developing. He had spent a long time talking to her about what their future would be like going forward and how he planned to make up for all the time he'd lost with her.

"We'll be a tight family," he told Deanne. "And make plans for the future together. You, me, and your mom."

Jen took a moment now to hug Lisa, hard. "Thank you so much for everything. You are a better friend than I deserve."

"Not at all," Lisa protested. "And it's only going to get better. Are you going to have to go back to Michigan to pack up your house?" She grinned. "I assume you won't be needing it anymore."

Jen shook her head. "I have to go back to meet with the FBI, and I can use the time to decide what I want to keep. We'll get rid of the rest, and Dino's hiring a firm to pack it and ship it."

"I'm so glad it all worked out. It's easy to see you

belong together. The three of you."

"We know that." She glanced over at Deanne who was clinging tightly to Dino's hand. "I really hit the jackpot, and I'm going to make sure nothing disrupts it. I love him, Lisa, he loves me, and we both love Deanne. That's all we need to make it work."

Seconds later, they were running to the helicopter. Dino boosted Deanne into the cabin before helping Jen and then pulling himself inside. He slid the door closed and nodded to Mike. They lifted off, banked, and headed south, the sun highlighting the landscape. He was explaining to Deanne how the helo worked, and she was listening in wide-eyed wonder.

"Think you'd like to live on the water in South Florida?" he asked now.

"Yes," she told him. "Do you have a boat?"

"I do. And we're going to spend a lot of time on it. The three of us. Me with my two very special girls."

As far as Jen was concerned, life could not get any better.

A word about the author…

USA Today best-selling and award-winning author Desiree Holt writes everything from romantic suspense and contemporary on a variety of heat levels up to erotic, a genre in which she is the oldest living author. She has been referred to by USA Today as the Nora Roberts of erotic romance and is a winner of the EPIC E-Book Award, the Holt Medallion, and a Romantic Times Reviewers Choice nominee. She has been featured on CBS Sunday Morning and in The Village Voice, The Daily Beast, USA Today, The (London) Daily Mail, The New Delhi Times and numerous other national and international publications.

~*~

Visit Desiree at
www.desireeholt.com

Also Available
from The Wild Rose Press, Inc.
and major retailers.

Finding Redemption
Guardian Security Book Five
By Desiree Holt

Lisa Mallory's marriage from hell ended with her husband's unsolved murder. Four years later, her eight-year-old son, Jamie, is kidnapped. When every other avenue of finding him fails, she turns to her brother's best friend. He's not the man she'd have chosen, but to get her son back, she'll suffer anything...even the desire he stirs that she'd thought long dead.

Ethan Caine, former Marine/special ops agent, is dealing with his own private hell. All he wants is to be left alone with a bottle of whiskey to drown the guilt of surviving a mission gone wrong. When he finally agrees to go after Jamie, he certainly doesn't want the boy's mother slowing him down. Besides, she makes him ache to have her naked and beneath him. Worse, she stirs dreams of the future...something he doesn't deserve.

Passion explodes between Ethan and Lisa in the exotic Quintana Roo jungle, even as the past and present threaten to steal it all.

This book was previously published under the title Redemption and has been heavily revised.

Also Available
from The Wild Rose Press, Inc.
and major retailers.

Pacific Persuasion

Australian Customs Security Romance Book One
Passport to Pleasure

By Sofia Aves

Head of security on the South Sea Mermaid, Kai Walker, hates having drugs on his ship. But when travelers begin to overdose and he can't find the source, Kai suspects everyone, including his absentee dinner partner, Pearl. He can't work out if she's a tempting distraction or an intentional diversion. He's keen to keep his threats close, even if it means a planned seduction to catch her in the act.

US DEA Agent Pearl Hamilton is determined to focus on the assignment she's been set. No sexy-as-sin security officer on a bewitching south sea cruise is going to turn her head, regardless of how good he looks in a uniform. That is, until she discovers how much fun she can have with a pair of handcuffs and a stolen room key…

Thank you for purchasing
this publication of The Wild Rose Press, Inc.

For questions or more information
contact us at
info@thewildrosepress.com.

The Wild Rose Press, Inc.
www.thewildrosepress.com